ROCK 'N' ROLL

Author's Preferred Edition

L. L. SOARES

He had no idea how she had been able to manipulate him into letting her stay, and how she had been able to excite him so strongly. During their lovemaking, he was once more amazed at the strange sensations he felt. It truly felt as if there was a mouth inside her, sucking him as she fucked him. It had to be some kind of trick, but she had never used it before, and no matter how hard he thought about it, he could not think of a logical explanation.

He went back to the bedroom and sat at the foot of the bed. There was a bottle by the bed with some wine left in it. He lifted it to his lips. "Lash."

It was a soft voice. Muffled. He turned to look at Lizzie, but she was still out cold.

"Lash, I'm over here."

The voice, strangely enough, seemed to be coming near Lizzie's legs. Her legs were spread apart as she slept, the sheets were on the floor, and Lash found his eyes focused between them. He saw something incredibly strange. Her vaginal lips were being pushed to the sides and what looked like a human tongue was sticking out of her.

Lizzie's lower abdomen was moving strangely, as if something was inside of her, moving around in there.

Lash put down the bottle and moved closer to where the tongue was. When he was close enough, it withdrew, back into Lizzie once more.

"Lash," the voice said, keeping the labia spread apart so it could speak to him.

"Come closer," the voice said, now that it had his attention. Something moved forward, toward him. A human mouth. Its lips were exposed, within Lizzie's vaginal lips.

"It's me," the mouth said.

"Who?" he whispered.

"Miranda."

For Kurt Newton

CHAPTER ONE

He was rocking back and forth, *against his will*, almost on the verge of losing consciousness, but he fought against it. He forced his eyes open and tried to focus.

He was staring at a photograph of a spotted pig. A fat white pig with large black spots. The spots were different shapes and sizes, like the ink blot tests psychiatrists use, and he almost put himself in a trance staring at them the way he did. The magazine he held felt gritty in his fingers, and the pages were crinkled. Many were torn.

Beneath the photograph was the legend: Bertha, First Prize.

Lash turned the page, and there was a photograph of a baby chick emerging from its shell that caught his eye.

He could hear the rain tapping on the wooden door of the gas station men's room.

Lash forced himself to stop rocking and closed the magazine. He put it down on the floor, beside the toilet. Then he got up from where he was sitting on the closed toilet lid, raised the lid, and took a long piss. He stared at the scrawlings on the wall in front of him. All of them were too smudged to read.

The room smelled of piss and shit, along with the acrid stench of vomit. For a moment, the smells threatened to engulf him. Smother him.

Someone banged on the door. "Do you know what time it is?"

Lash flushed the toilet and washed his hands. The paper towel dispenser was empty, and he had to wipe his wet hands on his jeans.

He opened the door. A man was standing outside, in the rain, tapping his watch with his index finger.

"Do you have any idea what time it is?" the man shouted.

"No."

"My watch stopped."

"Sorry to hear it," Lash said. He had the key to the men's room in his hand. It was attached to a big, square piece of wood. Lash handed the key to the man and pushed past him, walking back toward the car.

Miranda was sitting in the driver's seat, looking bored.

"It's about time you got done in there," she said, as he approached the car.

"I had to wait awhile to get in," he told her.

"I didn't see any line," she said. Then, "Get inside."

He got inside. She started the engine and drove away.

"I want to get there before six o'clock," she told him, when they were back on the highway. "You didn't have to take so long in there, did you?"

He didn't want to say anything to her about feeling sick. She had been planning this weekend for a long time.

"When you gotta go, you gotta go," he said.

She was tapping the steering wheel with her fingers. An annoying habit.

He reached over and turned on the radio.

When they had been driving for about half an hour, he asked her to pull over. He got out of the car and walked down an embankment, where there was grass and trees, and vomited all over the ground.

When he stopped, he wiped his mouth with his handkerchief and walked back up to the car.

"What's wrong with you?" she asked him.

"Motion sickness," he explained, getting back into the car.

Miranda stepped on the gas and drove on.

A little way ahead, they passed a man who had pulled his car over to the side of the road. It was a Cadillac. The man was dressed in a tuxedo, and he was running. But he didn't make it to where he was going and began to vomit all over his fancy suit.

"Looks like it's contagious," Miranda said.

CHAPTER TWO

They were sitting in the dining room, eating. There were blurry photographs in frames on the walls. The one closest to their table showed a man holding a line, attached to which were several fish.

"How's your steak?" Miranda asked him.

"Fine." he told her. And it was. But he couldn't enjoy it. His stomach still didn't feel right, and every once in a while, he could still taste the putrid flavor of his own vomit. The gin just couldn't obliterate the taste completely. And he felt caged in this place. He hadn't really wanted to come here. It had been Miranda's idea. She had suggested that they get away for a weekend, do something different. But he hated hotels. He always felt uncomfortable in places like this. He hated not sleeping in his own bed.

She was finished eating. "I'll be right back," she told him.

She got up and walked toward the bathrooms.

He took a swallow from his glass, then ate a forkful of baby carrots.

The waiter stopped by his table.

"How is everything?" the man asked.

"Fine," Lash told him.

The man smiled and walked away.

When he decided he'd eaten enough, Lash ordered another gin and sat back in his chair, waiting for Miranda to return.

She came back with a strange woman and a man. The three of them were laughing as they approached the table.

"I was out in the lobby, when I bumped into Susan," Miranda explained. "We were roommates in college."

Introductions were made all around. The man's name was

Mark. He and Susan were engaged.

Lash hated meeting new people. He had a strong desire to get away. But wasn't that why they had come to this place? To get away from it all?

"Why don't you sit down with us?" Miranda asked the couple.

"Mark and I were just about to get a bite to eat, anyway," Susan said.

"Well, we're just about done eating," Miranda said, noticing that their plates had already been cleared away. "But you're welcome to join us for drinks."

Everyone sat down. Lash finished his drink and motioned for the waiter.

"So what do you do?" Mark asked.

"I'm between jobs right now," Lash told him, not really interested in discussing himself with a total stranger.

"That's too bad," Mark said, trying to sound concerned. It came off as insincere. "I'm in real estate, myself. So is Susan. That's how we met."

The waiter came over and took their order. Lash found himself zoning out.

The girls were talking. Bits of their conversation that Lash caught involved guys they'd dated in college.

"Excuse me a minute," Lash said. He got up and went to the bathroom.

On the way back, he stopped at the bar and took his time with another drink. When he was done, he went back to the table, where everyone was caught up in their conversation, oblivious to his absence. Which was fine with him.

"Listen," he said to Miranda. "I hate to be rude, but I'm dead tired. Mind if I just meet you back at the room?"

"No, not at all," Miranda said. But she seemed uncomfortable with his suggestion. She had obviously wanted to involve him in the conversation. She looked at him, and she knew it was a lost cause. "I'll be up soon."

"Take your time," he told her. "Nice to meet you both," he lied to Susan and Mark, and then left the dining room.

Miranda always had a knack when it came to being sociable. It was not something they shared. Sometimes he wondered how they got together in the first place. But they were compatible in other ways. And at least she never made a big deal when he skipped out on some scene that he found particularly excruciating.

He sat on the bed, watching porno movies on cable television, drinking from a flask he had packed in his suitcase.

Eventually, she returned from the dining room.

"I hadn't seen Susan in years," she told him. "It was nice to see them."

"So, they're staying here, too?"

"They're leaving in the morning," Miranda said. "They've already been here a few days. And they had plans for this evening, if that's what you were worried about. It was nice to see them, though. Susan hasn't changed a bit. And Mark reminds me of a guy she used to date in college. Same kind of personality."

"Yeah, nice," Lash said, not at all interested.

"*What* are you watching?"

"A sanitized skin flick," he told her. "All the genital shots have been edited out. It kind of defeats the purpose. Like making a talk show for mutes."

"Well, we didn't come here to watch television, anyway," she said. "We came here to get away from everything, remember?"

"Yeah," he said, getting up to shut off the television. "I was just passing time, waiting for you to get back."

"You're not mad I took so long, are you?"

"I don't give a fuck," Rack said. "I was just up here, vegging out anyway."

"You don't like this place, do you?"

"It's too early to tell," he said. "It takes me a while to get used to things, I guess. But, like you said, it's a change of pace. That's good enough for me."

"The food was good."

"Yeah, fine."

She got on the bed with him.

"How much is left in the flask?"

"See for yourself," he said, handing it to her.

She took a long drink. It was almost empty.

"I'm going to order up a bottle from room service," she told him. "You might as well turn the TV back on."

He leaned forward and turned it back on. A nude woman was singing.

"Nice tits," he said.

Miranda laughed. "Awful voice, though."

She picked up the phone and ordered a bottle of gin. Then she went into the bathroom and poured herself a nice, hot bath.

Lash stayed on the bed, staring at the television screen. When there was a knock at the door, he cringed, hoping it wasn't Miranda's friends. He was relieved to see the room service guy.

He looked down at the cart the man was wheeling. On it was a bottle of Tanqueray gin, a bottle of soda water, a bucket of ice, and two glasses.

He gave the man a tip and wheeled the cart inside the room.

"Pour me a drink and come in here," Miranda called from the bathroom.

He made sure the door was locked, and then he poured her a drink and brought it to her.

"Thanks," she said, taking the glass.

"Nice bath?" he asked.

"Why don't you come in with me?" she asked.

He nodded his head. "Maybe some other time."

"You're not mad at me, are you?" she asked. "About my friends."

"Listen, you don't give me a hard time for leaving, and I won't give you a hard time for staying. Okay?"

"Okay," she said.

"You almost done?"

"It's so nice in here," she said, pouting her lips.

"Fine," he said. He turned around and left.

He was sitting on the bed when she came out, wrapped in a towel.

"This was supposed to be something special," she said. "And we're off to a bad start."

"It's not too late to fix things," he told her.

Miranda went over to the door and checked it, to make sure it was locked. She was nervous about things like that.

Then she dropped the towel and climbed into bed.

CHAPTER THREE

Miranda dropped him off in front of his apartment building and drove away. She didn't have much time to get ready for work. It was early on a Monday morning, another week beginning. They had stayed at the hotel longer than they had planned, and now she was in a rush.

Lash looked up at the still-dark sky, then down at his watch. The numbers glowed in the dark. It was almost five o'clock. The sun would begin rising soon. Miranda's taillights were out of sight. He went inside.

He went upstairs and stopped in front of his door. He put his suitcase down on the floor and jiggled his keys, trying to find the right one in the dark hallway. The hall light must have burned out. Finally, he found the key and let himself in.

He moved slowly, feeling in the dark for the light switch. Gently, he put his suitcase down on the floor and closed the door.

Lash stood there, listening.

He walked to his bedroom.

Lash stood in the threshold. Listening to the noises in the dark.

Someone was sleeping in his bed, and it sure as fuck wasn't *Goldilocks*.

"Lizzie?" he asked softly from the doorway. Then, a little louder. "Lizzie, is that you?"

"Lash?" She sounded half asleep.

"Yeah."

"I hope you don't mind me sleeping here while you were gone," she said. A voice in the dark. But there were the noises, evidence that a body was attached to that voice. She was moving around. Ashamed of being caught. Nervous. "You told me you'd be gone this weekend."

"I know," he said. Trying his best not to be angry with her. Holding his tongue and trying not to berate her. To tell her that his being gone was not an invitation for her to come and stay there. She had her own place, after all. "The weekend's over," he said softly.

It was best to be gentle with her. To not make things worse than they were.

"You're alone, right?" she asked. "I didn't mess anything up, did I?"

You're messing up my whole fucking life, he thought. But he didn't say it.

"Yeah," he said. "I'm alone. But I'd prefer if you didn't pull this kind of thing anymore, okay? I don't like surprises as much as I used to."

Not that it was really a surprise. He had anticipated her being here. It was one of the things that made him hesitate every time Miranda hinted about their moving in together.

"Sure, Lash," she said, still hidden in the dark. "Whatever you say. You see, this was a special case. I locked myself out of my place, but I knew where you kept your spare key. And I knew you'd be gone."

He had to do something about that spare key. And he had to change the locks. But it wouldn't stop her from finding other ways to get in.

"How did you know I'd be gone until today?" he said. "I mean, I didn't know myself until the last minute."

"I just knew," she told him, sounding very sure. It almost unnerved him for a moment. This surety. Like she knew him better than he knew himself. He felt violated by that. He had no desire to maintain this level of intimacy.

"What if I wasn't alone right now?" he asked her. "Do you know how embarrassing that would be."

"I knew you'd be alone," Lizzie said. "She has to get ready for work."

You have all the answers, he thought, angrily. He resisted the urge to turn on the bedroom light. To confront her face to face.

"On your way out, leave the spare key with me. Okay?"

"Oh, you're angry."

"I'm not too bent out of a shape, but I want my key back, that's all."

"Okay," she assured him.

"So how are you going to get back into your apartment?"

"The landlord has another key, but it was too late to wake him when I got in last night. Besides, I'd been drinking, and I couldn't think straight."

"So you only slept here the one night?" he asked.

"That's all," she said. "I swear it."

He knew she was lying, that she had probably been here the whole weekend, but he let it go. There was no use accusing her. Making things worse than they already were.

He tried to say something, but his mouth was so dry. He found it hard to swallow. Then, somehow, he found his voice again. "Don't you have to leave soon?"

"It's still so early," she said. "Can I sleep a little bit more?"

"Sure," he told her. He closed the bedroom door and went back to the living room. He turned on the television. There was an old black-and-white horror movie on. He turned off the lamp and sat down in the chair in front of the television. Watching.

The apartment was very quiet, except for the soft sounds coming from the television. A woman on screen was screaming, but the volume was down low.

Lash sat there, watching. Trying to concentrate on what was on the screen. But his mind was on other things.

The window shade in the room was up a crack, and he could see the sun was rising.

A horrible face pressed up against the television screen and growled. At first, it looked realistic, but the longer it stayed on-screen, the phonier it looked. The woman was still screaming, but she was off-screen now.

Then it went to a commercial.

He didn't hear it when Lizzie came up behind him. She put a hand on his shoulder.

Lash turned around.

"I tried to get back to sleep, but I couldn't," she explained.

She was dressed in his bathrobe. The one he never wore. "Have you got anything for breakfast around here? I'll make us something."

"All I've got is cereal," he told her. "If there's any left. If you want, I could go to the store down the street and pick up some eggs and bacon."

"No," she said. "Don't bother doing that."

He looked into her face. She had that look. That desperate look. It pained him to see it, but he didn't show it. He had no intention of giving into her.

"I'd better get ready to go," she told him. "I've been too much trouble already. Are you still mad at me?"

"No," he said.

"I'm sorry I came here, slept here, without asking you first. But I was in a fix, like I told you."

"I know, I know," he said, getting exasperated. He just wanted her to leave.

She let the robe slip open, and he turned around again and went back to watching the television.

"I'd better go," she said. She resisted an urge to touch his arm again.

"Do you have to use the shower?" he asked, then cursed himself. It opened a door he didn't want to enter. But she didn't use it. She let him off the hook this time.

"No, I'll wait until I get back home," she said. "I have to change my clothes, anyway."

She went back to the bedroom, and he could hear her getting dressed. She made as much noise as she could.

He was still staring at the television. Cartoons were on, now. He watched, but his mind didn't really register the images.

She came back into the living room. "Well, thanks for the place to stay," she said. "Call me sometime."

"Bye," he said, not turning to look at her.

She opened the door and left. He realized, as she closed the door, that he hadn't asked her again for the key back. But he resisted going after her. He didn't want to look into her eyes again.

He would just have to get it back some other time.

Lash got up and locked the door. Then he went over to a window and raised the shade.

The sun was rising higher in the sky. After a few minutes, he heard a sound below and knew she was down there, on the sidewalk. But he didn't look down.

Instead, he decided he really needed more sleep and went to bed.

CHAPTER FOUR

Lash was shivering in bed, trying to clear his mind of all thoughts.

After Lizzie left, he had gotten sick again. He had stayed in the bathroom for about an hour, holding on to the toilet bowl, heaving every now and then. At one point, he thought it would never end.

What the fuck is wrong with me, he wondered. *I must be coming down with some kind of bug.*

Miranda had called that morning, when she was at work. He wasn't going to answer the phone, but when he heard her voice on the answering machine, he dragged himself over. He tried to talk her out of coming over that night. It might be contagious.

But she insisted on seeing him, as he knew she would.

So he went back to bed and waited.

The vomiting had stopped, and he just curled up in a ball, shivering. There were stretches when he would lose consciousness, and then he would wake up again in the dark room. All the shades were pulled down.

At the end of the day, he heard the front door open, and Miranda's voice called out, "Why is it so cold in here?"

She removed her coat and stood in the doorway of his bedroom.

"How are you feeling?" she asked.

"The same."

"I turned up the heat," she said. "Someone has to nurse you through this thing."

"I told you not to bother," he said. "I can handle it."

"Bullshit," she said. "I want to take care of you."

She sat on the bed next to him and touched him. She could feel him shivering.

"You *are* sick," she said. "I think maybe I should stay overnight."

"You don't have to," he said. "I took care of myself all day. All I really need is some sleep."

"Do you want anything to eat?" she asked. "You have to try and eat something."

"Some soup," he said, trying to sit up. "That's all I can stomach."

"Sure," she said, getting up and disappearing into the growing darkness.

A light came on down the hall, where the kitchen was, and he stared at it. He could hear her moving about in there, and he listened intently to the sounds she made. She didn't move like Lizzie did. Miranda was more fluid, the sounds she made more comforting, reassuring.

After a time, she returned, and put a tray on his lap. On the tray, was a bowl of soup. Despite the fact that he had been sick most of the day, he was hungry, and he ate the soup as quickly as he could.

"Whoa," Miranda said, watching him eat. "I'm not going to take it away from you."

"I didn't realize how hungry I was," Lash told her.

"That's a good sign, at least," she said.

When he was done, she took the tray away.

"Do you want anything else?" she asked him.

"No, really, I think all I need is some more sleep."

"You sure you don't want me to stick around?" she asked. "I can always sleep on the couch if you want."

"No," he said. "It will be boring for you. All I'm going to do is sleep. What do you want to stick around for?"

"You know," she said, "sometimes I think you're trying to push me away."

"You know that's not true."

"Do I?" she said. "If I lived here, I could take care of you right."

"I don't need anyone to take care of me."

"Is that so?" she asked. "Have you eaten anything all day before I got here?"

"No," he admitted. "I didn't even know I was hungry until you gave me that soup."

"That proves my point," she said. "Do you ever even think about moving in together?"

"Of course I do," he said. "You mention it often enough."

"Don't you want to?" she said. "Huh? We're so good for each other."

"I know we are," Lash said. "I just don't know if I'm ready to give up all my privacy just yet. I'm used to living alone. I kind of like it."

That wasn't totally true, but he really didn't want to discuss it just then.

Miranda looked disappointed. "Okay, if you really want me to go, I'll go."

"I don't want you to go," Lash said. "But I want to get some sleep. I won't get any if you're here."

"I won't argue with you about it," she said. "How are you feeling now? Do you want anything else to eat?"

"I'm fine," he said. He rolled over under the covers. "Just shut off all the lights before you go, okay?"

She went over to him and leaned over. She kissed him.

"I'm going to call you tomorrow," she said.

"Sure."

She hesitated and then left the room. She put on her coat and then started turning off lights.

"Bye," she called out. "You make sure you get plenty of sleep."

"Bye," he said.

Then she was gone. He sat up in bed, in the dark, listening.

A spasm came over him without warning. He vomited all over himself, the sheets, and the bed. It seemed unstoppable, and then, as suddenly as it began, it stopped.

He tried to get out of bed, but he was so exhausted, all he could do was close his eyes and sleep.

CHAPTER FIVE

L ash woke to the sound of the phone ringing. He got out of bed, feeling better than he had in weeks. But the stink of the room was awful. He ran to the living room to answer the phone.

It was Miranda.

"How do you feel this morning?" she asked.

"Better," he said. "A lot better. I knew that sleep would do me good. That's all I needed."

"I was going to come by this morning, before I went to work, and check on you, but I didn't want to wake you up."

"That's good," he said. "Because I slept late."

"Do you want me to come over tonight?" she asked.

"Sure," he said. "That sounds great. Let's go out somewhere to eat."

"Okay," she said. "I'll treat."

"It doesn't matter," he said. "I just want to see you."

She sounded happy. "I'll come by after work."

"Great."

"Bye," she said. "Love you."

"Bye," he said, and hung up the phone.

He went back to the bedroom. He rolled up all the sheets and stuck them in a laundry bag. He tried to wash things as well as he could, and then he took a shower and put on fresh clothes.

He burned some incense and then went out to do the laundry.

When he got back, the place smelled a little better.

The phone rang.

"Hello," he said.

It was a client.

"I'll be there in about an hour," he said.

CHAPTER SIX

They had cleared space for him on the floor.

In fact, the room was devoid of furniture, except for a bed, which was low to the ground, on one side of the room.

Lash removed his clothes and got down on the cold wood floor. He closed his eyes.

His clients, a man and a woman, got into the bed, and began to touch one another.

Lash slowly rocked back and forth on the floor.

His mind was a jumble of images. There were faces, body parts, spotted pigs, and chicks breaking out of shells.

The clients began to fuck.

Lash rolled around on the floor more violently. It looked as if he were having a fit. But he wasn't in any discomfort. He was in a kind of a trance.

The more he moved about on the floor, the more the sensations his clients felt were enhanced.

Their sensations were increased and prolonged.

He was like a conductor, leading a symphony to higher and higher crescendos. He would slow down at points, and then built things up again. The couple on the bed were like puppets, reacting as he pulled their sexual strings.

The whole process lasted a couple of hours. They made a lot of noise. That was normal. His clients tended to get very caught up in what was happening to them.

Lash was silent as he rocked and rolled.

When it was over, the three of them stopped moving and rested for a while. Then, when he felt able, Lash got up from the floor and got dressed. He had an erection. He often did when it was over. Very seldom did he reach orgasm himself during these sessions.

The couple in bed did not move. They were locked in each other's arms. He could barely hear their breathing.

On a table outside the room, there was an envelope. Lash took it, counted the money inside, and put it in his wallet.

Then he left.

CHAPTER SEVEN

When Lash got back to his apartment, Lizzie was waiting for him again.

She was sitting in the chair in front of the television, watching a game show.

"What are you doing here?" he asked her.

"Just get back from a job?" she asked him.

"You didn't answer my question."

"You wanted your key back," she said. "I came by to give it back. You weren't here, so I thought I'd wait for you."

"You couldn't just slip it under the door?"

"I wanted to do it in person," she told him. "I wanted to say again how sorry I am."

"How did you know I would be back this early," he said. "I could've been gone longer."

"I knew."

"Bullshit!"

"Look, if you took too long, I would have left. I could always come back again later."

"You could have just left the key and a note," he said.

"I wanted to do it in person," she said.

Lizzie got up from the chair. She was wearing a dress that accentuated her attributes. She was still a very attractive woman, after all.

"So," she said. "Do you want your key back or not?"

"I want it," he said. "And I want you to leave. I have a lot to do, and I don't have time right now for a visit."

"You're in a bad mood," she said. "You're sweating, too. You must have just come from a job."

He held out his hand for the key.

"How about I stay and give you a massage," she said. "You could probably use it just about now. Does all that rolling around still play havoc with your back? I remember you'd get bruises sometimes, too."

"I need a hot bath, that's all."

"How about I scrub you down," she said, with a smile. "Like the old days."

"Listen," he said. "Your lunch hour must be over. Don't you have somewhere to be?"

"Not really," she said. "I'm all yours, if you want me."

"Well, I *don't*," he said. "Or didn't you get the hint when we got divorced?"

"That was a long time ago. And we've managed to stay friends all these years. Haven't we? Sometimes, it's more than friends. Besides, I know someday you'll break down and realize that we belong together."

"That's not very likely," he said. "Considering that I'm involved with someone else now."

"Miranda's nice and all, but we have a bond. A real bond. Something like a divorce can't break a bond like we've got. It's something spiritual, baby."

"That's what you say," Lash said. "What I say is that it's time for you to leave."

"You don't want to go into the bedroom?" she asked. "I remember you used to be pretty horny sometimes after a job."

"I'm just real tired right now, and I don't have the patience for this shit. I made it clear what I want. Now give me the key."

She got up and reached into her purse. She handed him the key.

"Maybe now we won't have any more unexpected visits," he told her.

"Yeah, yeah."

"I have things to do. How's about giving me my space?"

She got closer and touched his arm. Her confrontational manner dissolved. Her face was vulnerable. He expected her to beg, but she controlled herself.

"I didn't mean to get you mad, Lash," she said. "Please don't be mad at me."

"Yeah, well don't push me."

"I wouldn't want you to stay mad at me," she said. "I couldn't stand it."

"Well, if you leave right now, you won't have to worry about it."

She went to the door. "I can still drop by and visit you sometimes, can't I?"

"Just make sure you call first," he said.

"Sure," she said. "I'll call first."

She opened the door and turned to look back at him one last time. He scowled at her. She left.

Lash closed the door and locked it. Then he attached the chain lock.

He then went to the bathroom and turned on the bath water.

CHAPTER EIGHT

They stayed in and ordered a pizza.

Both were drinking beer, which was unusual for Miranda because she was always watching her figure. She admitted to him that she liked the taste of it, though.

When the pizza delivery man came, Miranda was going to pay, but Lash stopped her. "I got paid today," he told her.

When they were eating, Lash couldn't help noticing that Miranda was on edge, debating in her head whether or not she should bring the matter up. They'd discussed it several times. What he did for a living. He didn't tell her what he really did. Instead, he said that he got odd jobs every now and then. He didn't like to go into detail, because he didn't like to have to lie.

He tried to avoid the whole subject. He had been avoiding it since they first met. When she had asked him what kind of work he did, he had always been evasive. At one point, he told her he was a freelance writer, he even bought a laptop to complete the illusion, but she never saw him write, and he never had any manuscript pages to show her. He knew she didn't believe that story anymore.

She suspected that he was doing something illegal, even though she never really came out with it, and it bothered her. It worried her.

Someday he would tell her, but it wasn't the right time. They'd been going out about five months, and he didn't know if he trusted her enough, yet.

He kept telling himself he did, but at the last minute he would hesitate.

She ate three slices of the pizza quicker than he did.

"Boy, you sure got an appetite tonight."

"So you worked today, huh?"

"Today? No, not really. I wanted to rest up, make sure I was feeling okay. I got paid for some work I did last week."

"What kind of work?"

"Do we have to talk about this?" he asked. "I really want to enjoy being together."

"Why don't you ever want to talk about it?" she asked.

"It's not really interesting, that's all," he told her. "I do things like clean out apartments for people who want to rent them out. Stuff like that, for friends of mine. It's not very exciting, but it's some money every now and then."

"So you don't write anymore?"

"Naw, I haven't written in a while."

She let that go. She wasn't going to call him on it.

"Do you ever think about finding something steady?" she asked him. "A real job?"

"I'm doing okay."

"Lash, I'm serious about this. I worry about you sometimes."

"You don't have to," he said. "I'm doing fine. I always pay my bills. I've never once asked you for money. I always pay my own way."

"I know," she said. "But I worry anyways."

He wanted to tell her, he wanted so badly. But then he thought of Lizzie. He didn't want Miranda to be like her. He wanted to hold it off for as long as he could.

I should have told her something a long time ago. Something good. But I don't have any imagination, he thought.

"Listen, I was never cut out for the whole nine-to-five thing," he said. "It's not for me. I do okay. I always have work. And it's a lot easier than suffering, being trapped in an office like an animal in a cage."

"I work in an office," she said. "It isn't that bad."

"I know, I know," he said. "You don't mind it that much. But I'm different."

"I feel trapped sometimes, too," she said. "More than you'd think. But I handle it."

"Can we talk about something else?" he asked.

She got up and went to the bathroom. He watched television and finished his beer.

He had really wanted to tell her the truth. But he didn't know how. He was afraid of her reaction.

She was in the bathroom longer than he thought she should be. He went over to check on her. Standing by the door, he thought he heard her heaving inside.

"Miranda, are you okay?"

"Go away."

He went back to the sofa. He grabbed another slice of pizza from the box. He opened a fresh bottle of beer.

Miranda came back.

"You must have caught what I had," he said.

"I hope not," she said. "I can't afford to get sick."

"I suppose you're not hungry anymore, huh?"

"Let's go to bed," she said.

CHAPTER NINE

As they made love, he shook his body a little, but he could never build up the momentum he got when he rolled around on the floor. It was enough to give her a taste, however.

She just thought he was really good in bed.

He wanted to give her the full job. Get her screaming. But he would think of Lizzie and he would hold back.

Lizzie was an addict. He had made her that way. It was his fault she had become so hooked on him. Coming around all the time, trying to talk him into doing it just one more time. And he gave in now and then, because he felt sorry for her. Because he knew it was his fault, that he had ruined her for other men.

Him and some crazy talent he had, that he had never asked for, that sometimes he didn't even want.

Looking down into Miranda's face, listening to her soft, breathy sounds, he wanted to give her the full treatment. But he didn't want to change what they had. He wanted a normal relationship. He wanted to try to have a normal life.

How long can I keep this up? he wondered. *How much longer can I live a lie?*

CHAPTER TEN

"Do you want anything to drink?" Antony asked.

Lash was standing by the window of the penthouse apartment, looking down at the city below. They were sixty flights up.

"No, thanks," he asked. "I don't like to drink before a job."

"I invited you a little early," Antony said. "I've had you over here a few times now, and we've never really talked before."

"Do we have to?" Lash asked. He had never had much of a desire to know his clients too well. It made things easier to maintain a distance from his work.

"No," Antony said. He was in his early thirties. He had probably thought he was pretty jaded before he discovered what Lash could do. "We don't have to. But I have to admit that I've been very curious about you. About what goes on inside your head."

"The same kinds of things that go on inside anyone else's head," Lash said, still staring out the big window.

"I doubt it," Antony said. "Everyone thinks about different things. We all have different lives."

Lash grunted.

"What does it feel like when you do it?"

"Do it?" Lash asked, even though he knew full well what his client meant.

"That rolling around. Is it painful, or does it give you some kind of high? Or does it get you off or something?"

"None of the above," Lash said. "Not really. To tell the truth, I really don't feel much of anything. I kind of go numb."

"That doesn't sound so good," Antony said. "I was hoping that maybe you felt it, too."

"No, I don't," Lash said. "Unfortunately."

"Does it ever get frustrating for you? Affecting others this way, and not getting to enjoy it?"

"Frustrating? I guess I never really thought about it before. It's not really all that bad. Like I said, it's like a numbness. Like being in a trance. Nothing too awful."

"Do you get to enjoy a normal sex life?" Antony asked.

"Now we're talking about stuff I'm not sure I want to discuss," Lash said. "Let's just say I'm happy and leave it at that."

"Of course," Antony said. He looked at his watch. It was shiny and gold. "She said she would be here by now. I hope she isn't going to stand us up."

She must be a new one, Lash thought. If she had done this before, she wouldn't be late.

"Do you want anything to eat? Are you hungry? I have plenty of food."

"No," Lash said. "I'm fine."

The phone rang. Antony went into the kitchen to answer it.

Lash looked out the window, imagining what it would be like to fall from this height. To feel the wind slapping at him, pressure roaring in his ears.

Antony was talking loudly in the other room, but Lash did not want to hear the conversation. He heard the noises, but he didn't concentrate on the words. He just kind of blocked them out.

Antony came back in. "She's not going to show up, the bitch! She waits until the last minute to let me know she can't make it."

"Did she know I was going to be here?"

"No, it was a surprise. I wanted to really freak her out, you know. She never experienced anything like this before. I tried to tell her over the phone, how she was really missing out on something, but she wouldn't listen. I had the whole thing planned out—for nothing!"

He was very upset. Lash didn't know what to say to calm him down.

"She has no idea what she's missing," Antony said. "I was going to let her in on this, but now I'm going to reconsider the whole thing, you know? Fuck her! I don't need her."

This was strange for Lash. People didn't normally miss a chance to have him do his thing.

"Well, since you came all the way out here, let's say we stop wasting your time."

"You want to go forward with this?"

"I guess I should call someone else," Antony said. "But, you see, I don't want to share this with just anyone. I don't know if I can reach anyone else I trust on such short notice."

"So what do you want to do?"

"Don't worry, you'll work. You'll get paid."

"I'm ready when you are," Lash said.

"Let me make some calls," Antony said. "I'll pay you for your time."

"Whatever."

Antony went into the other room and made some calls.

Lash looked around at the expensively furnished apartment. He had been here a few times. He remembered once, Antony shot up some heroin and asked Lash to do his thing, to increase the high. Lash had started out, but he stopped after a short time. He was terrified that Antony would go into overdose mode. What he did worked for sex, but drugs were something else. Lash couldn't be sure about the consequences. He refused to go on and Antony never asked him to do it again.

For some reason, he wasn't angry about Lash's refusal. He called him again soon afterward to make another appointment.

Antony came back into the room. "Well, I got ahold of someone," he said. "She'll be right here."

Lash nodded.

"You sure you don't want anything," Antony said. "Anything at all?"

"No," Lash said. "I'm fine. Really."

"Did you ever think about that offer I made?" Antony asked. "I have some friends who would be very interested in what you have to offer."

"I haven't decided yet."

"What's to decide?" Antony asked. Then, he realized that Lash wasn't going to answer. "Well, think about it, okay?"

Lash nodded.

The phone rang. Antony answered it. Lash heard him say, "Send her up."

"I'd rather pay you now," Antony said. "How much do I owe you?"

Lash quoted a price.

"Fine," Antony said. He wrote out a check and handed it to Lash.

Lash put the check in his wallet and put the wallet away. The elevator doors opened and a tall brunette came in. He recognized her from one of the earlier sessions. She was a model. He had seen her in magazine ads for perfume and jeans.

She was wearing just a silk bathrobe. It stretched down to her shins and had faux fur trim around the collar.

"Hi," she said, smiling at Lash. Then she grabbed Antony's outstretched hands.

"Darling, thank you so much for thinking of me," she said, kissing Antony on the lips. "I was wondering when I was going to get to do this again."

"That bitch Essie was supposed to show, and she didn't," Antony said. "So she's out and you're in, babe!"

It didn't seem to bother her that he had asked someone else first. "Excellent! Her loss in my gain."

She took off the bathrobe. She was naked underneath.

"I came prepared," she said, smiling again at Lash.

Lash smiled back. He didn't say anything.

Her body was beautiful. Lash knew that, if he had the desire to, he could easily hook up with some of these women. But he felt weird coming on to clients. It was unprofessional. Besides, he had Miranda waiting for him, and she was no slouch in the looks department, either.

And he thought that maybe he was falling in love with her.

I think I'm going to ask her to move in with me soon, he thought. *Hell, I might tell her everything, too. Lay it all out on the table.*

"Are you ready?" Antony asked.

He followed them into the bedroom. The model undressed Antony. Lash undressed himself and got down on the lush carpet.

He could hear them begin behind him.

He closed his eyes and began as well.

After a time, all he could hear was the beating of his heart.

CHAPTER ELEVEN

The phone kept ringing and ringing, but Lash didn't pick it up.

He's not home, she thought. *He must be at a job.*

Lizzie put the phone down and paced back and forth. She was getting impatient. She had to see him again. Soon.

On the wall, there were pictures of him. If he ever found out about it, he would probably bug out. She wasn't living up to her part of the deal.

Before the divorce, they had really talked about things, and they had a verbal agreement. Just the two of them knew about it. He had agreed to see her occasionally, as long as she didn't get too obsessive about the whole thing. But she couldn't help herself. She thought about him constantly.

Maybe the way he was so civil about the whole thing made him more desirable to her and made the whole thing harder to deal with. If he had been heartless, and he had cut her out of his life completely, then maybe she could have moved on with her own life. Quit him cold turkey. But, with things the way they were, the bond they shared was still there. For her, it was stronger than ever.

But Lash was getting closer to Miranda, and he had less and less patience for her. Something was bound to happen. Something that Lizzie had been dreading for quite some time.

She had never wanted to divorce him, but she had agreed to it out of fear that he would cut her off completely. He felt sorry for her. She had to use that to get whatever she could get.

He once told her that she scared him. She couldn't understand that at all.

Couldn't he see that she loved him?

But he hadn't cut her off, not yet. That was a good sign, she had convinced herself. And they did have that verbal agreement. It had been the only way she would have agreed to the divorce at all.

Lizzie picked up the phone again and punched out his number. The phone began to ring.

Five. Six. Seven times.

No answer.

Instead of hanging up, she leaned against the wall and waited.

The ringing of the phone became a kind of music for her, and it lulled her. But then she kind of woke up and realized what she was doing, and she hung the phone up.

I hope he gets back soon, she thought. *I wonder why his answering machine isn't working.*

She paced back and forth. Back and forth. Like a caged animal.

She was a lioness, fully aware of the dimensions of her cage, waiting for her chance to escape.

CHAPTER TWELVE

When Lash got home, the phone was ringing. His first instinct was not to pick it up, but for some reason he did.

It was Lizzie.

"Lash, is that you?"

"Yeah, Lizzie, what is it?"

"How come your answering machine isn't working?"

"I must have shut it off and forgot to turn it back on," he said. "What's so important?"

"I have to see you, Lash."

"Look, Lizzie, we've talked about this before…"

"I've tried to be cool about it, but I've got to see you."

He wanted to tell her to fuck off, but he figured it would be best to deal with the situation in a more subtle way. It might be better if they spoke in person.

"Okay," he told her. "It's still early in the afternoon. Give me time to take a shower. How about I come over there for a change?"

She hesitated. "Let's meet somewhere neutral. How about a hotel room?"

"I don't have time to set that up," he said. "Look, if you don't want to get together…"

She was going to ask him what was wrong with his place, but she wanted to play it cool. "I'll take care of all the details. I'll call you right back. Take your shower."

"Okay," he said, not liking it at all, but wanting to get off the phone.

"And turn your answering machine back on."

"Yeah, yeah," he said, and hung up.

Seeing Lizzie was the last thing he wanted to do, and he had really wanted to tell her to forget it. But he had decided it was time to resolve this whole thing, once and for all, before it got out of hand. Closure was long overdue.

He was sweaty and had a bad headache. He went to the bathroom and opened the medicine cabinet. He took some aspirin.

After he washed down the pills, he turned on the shower and got undressed.

He wasn't in the mood to see anyone. He just wanted to be left alone. And he definitely had no desire to see another hotel room right now.

Lizzie was really getting on his nerves lately. He was almost starting to hate her.

As hot water washed over him, his mind wandered.

I divorced the bitch, for Christ's sake, he thought. *I don't owe her anything anymore. Why can't she just leave me alone? Why does she always have to make demands on me? And why do I keep giving in to her?*

He tried to let go of these things and let his mind go blank. All he was aware of was the hot water pounding on his flesh. He lathered himself up and washed the sweat away.

When he was done, he found a message on his answering machine, from Lizzie, letting him know where they were going to meet.

CHAPTER THIRTEEN

When he got there, Lizzie was already drinking. She offered him some wine as he came in the door.

"What do you want?" he asked her.

"You know," she said.

"No, I don't know," he said. "Tell me."

"I want you to *do* me."

"Look, I just got done with a job," he said. "It was really exhausting. I don't like to do that more than once a day. It drains the hell out of me."

"We used to make love all the time after you got back from a job," she said.

"You're not asking me to make love. Not really."

"Please, Lash," she said. "I've tried to be patient. I've waited so long."

It had been a couple of weeks. She *had* been patient, for her, even though she always seemed so anxious, so on edge. But he wanted to end this completely. End it forever.

"Listen, I'm involved with Miranda now. I don't have time for you anymore. You and your begging and pleading. You have to learn to get on without me, to get on with your life. You have to do it cold turkey."

"I can't, Lash."

"I can't keep giving in to you. You know that. I have to just say no and end this whole thing. You have to accept it."

"We have an agreement," she said. "You promised me."

"I know," he said. "And I've lived up to that agreement for a long time now. Too long, in fact. And now it's time to move on. For *both* of us to move on. You understand that, don't you? It's not healthy for either one of us anymore."

"Don't think of me as your ex-wife. Think of me as a client. Hell, I'll even pay you if that's what you want."

Lash drank from his wine glass. Then, "I don't think so, Lizzie."

"One last time," she pleaded. "And then I'll leave you alone."

He didn't know what to say. He wanted nothing to do with this, but she was so needy.

"Okay," he said, knowing that he was caving in yet again, that he was making a sham of everything he just said. "But this is the last time. That's it."

Why do I always give in to her?

Her neediness was one of the main reasons why had had to break things off between them in the first place. Not that things had changed much since the divorce. She still stayed in touch, and she still begged to spend time with him. Begged to feel the enhancement thing. *Just one more time.* Snowballing into hundreds of times.

There were a few times when she had seemed on the verge of rebuilding her life, but she consistently failed. It was a burden for him to realize that giving in to her was a way of perpetualizing her failure. She saw him as an object, and he had reinforced it each time he gave into her wants, making it harder and harder to convince her that he was a human being with wants and needs of his own. Wants and needs that no longer included her.

At least she had eased up enough in the past year or so, enough so that he could try to have a real relationship with another woman. He had found Miranda, and even seemed to be maintaining something lasting with her, and throughout it Lizzie had not gone out of her way to break them apart. Sure, there were a few close calls, when Lizzie had arrived unannounced, and had somehow gotten ahold of a copy of his key, but it was nothing like the period just after they got divorced. Then, she refused to let him out of her sight, and he made things harder for them both by letting her hold on. Sometimes, it felt like the divorce really hadn't happened at all.

Guilt had a lot to do with it. He discovered he had the ability to enhance others' sensations quite by accident, in the early years of their marriage. She was the first one he had ever done it to. It had not manifested itself before that. And she had always had an addictive personality. Deep inside, he felt responsible for her need, and he felt that he owed her something. And she had never done anything all that harmful, except beg and plead and grasp.

But her begging and pleading and grasping were a form of abuse in themselves, he now realized. She had terrorized him with her neediness for a long time.

All of this went through his mind as he went with her to the bedroom.

"Right off the bat," he told her, laying down the law. "I want to make something clear. No physical contact."

"Aw, come on," she said. "Just one last time."

"No," he said. "I'm involved with Miranda now. I'm not interested."

"Since when did you become a prude?" she asked. "It's not like you and I are strangers in the bedroom. We fucked after the last time, if you remember, and that wasn't very long ago."

"No physical contact," he repeated. "That's the one condition I have. Take it or leave it."

"Okay," she said. "Whatever you want."

She got on the bed.

He realized he still had the wine glass in his hand. He drained it and put it in the other room.

When he came back into the room, Lizzie was already undressed. Her body hadn't changed much over the years. She had gotten a little thinner. She kept in real good shape, and she didn't show any noticeable signs of age. For all he knew, she kept in good shape just for him. It wasn't like she was going out of her way to have any other lasting relationships, after all. As far as he knew, she hadn't even dated anyone since they broke up.

He turned around and watched her touch herself. Her eyes were closed.

She had been drinking before he arrived, too. She wanted two highs for the price of one.

Watching her fondle herself, he couldn't help but feel aroused. She touched herself in the most passionate ways, and she was clearly enjoying it.

He did not want to touch her, though. He wanted to keep his distance. Otherwise, he would risk falling back into her trap. The trap of guilt and emotional blackmail. If he was going to loosen the bonds between them, he had to start now.

It was long overdue.

Her fingers continued to explore the region between her legs. Her head was tossed back, her dyed blonde hair sprayed across the pillows.

He turned his back to her. Then he got undressed. It made things easier and more comfortable. He folded his clothes and put them to one side, then he stretched out on the floor and started rolling.

Although he went into a kind of a trance during these things, he couldn't help hearing the noises she made, the volume turned up somewhere inside his head, as he rolled.

When he came out of the trance, he stopped moving. He didn't know what let him know it was over. He just came out of it and was done. He lay on the carpet for a few minutes, trying to catch his breath. Then he sat up and turned to face her.

She was curled in a ball on the bed, breathing loudly. This was normally the time when he would crawl into bed with her. But that's not how it went this time. Instead, he watched her for a few minutes, then he got up and got dressed.

She opened her eyes and lifted her head so she could see him. He saw her move and looked at her.

"That was wonderful," she said.

He didn't have anything to say in response; he continued to get dressed in silence. He didn't want to say anything that could be misconstrued as sharing intimacy between them. She was just another client. She had to be made aware that this was the end, that it was now over between them.

"Are you sure I can't do anything for you?" she asked.

He left the room.

He poured himself another glass of wine and went over to the couch. Every now and then he looked in the direction of the bedroom.

When he was almost done, she came out of the bedroom.

She hadn't bothered to dress. The odor of her sex was strong on her.

"Thank you," she said, still trying to catch her breath. "I know you really didn't want to do that, and I…I'm sorry about that."

He grunted. Then, "It's okay," he said. "As long as you realize this is the last time. The absolute last time."

"I know," she said. "I get the message."

"Good."

He wasn't looking at her.

"Can we still be friends?"

"Sure," he said, feeling like he was acting in a play. Hadn't they had this conversation a hundred times before? "But nothing more, get it?"

"Got it."

He stared down at his empty glass. He thought about refilling it again, but he really just wanted to get the hell out of there.

"I have to go," he said.

"I have to admit, I hate to see you go," she said.

He stood up. "Bye," he said.

"I want to wish you lots of happiness with Miranda. I can tell you really care about her deeply."

Lizzie sounded very sincere.

"Thanks," Lash said, looking into her eyes.

He left. In a strange way, he felt a kind of regret in leaving her there. He regretted not touching her when they were in the bedroom. At the same time, he was very relieved that the whole thing was over.

Now, maybe he could go on with his life.

How many times had he tried to end it before? She seemed so sincere this time, as if she finally was able to accept the fact that things were over between them. But how could he be sure?

Only time would tell.

Time. He looked at his watch. It was getting late. Miranda would be getting out of work soon. He had just enough time to get back and take another shower.

CHAPTER FOURTEEN

"You know, I've been thinking," Lash said. "How would you like to move in here?"

"I thought you said this place was too small," Miranda said. She was wearing one of his T-shirts, from an Alice Cooper concert he went to years ago, and it was way too big for her. Maybe she had lost more weight.

"On second thought, it will be real cozy, then," he said. "And you won't have to travel back and forth all the time. Listen, if you want, we could do it as an experiment. You know, a trial run. If it doesn't work out, we can change our minds."

"It sounds intriguing," she admitted.

"Good, then will you think about it?"

"Sure."

They were on the sofa, and when he pulled her over his knees, the T-shirt rode up so he could see her ass. She wasn't wearing anything else.

He got the urge to spank her. Not hard, just enough to startle her.

"What are you doing?" she said, laughing.

"I'm trying to speed up your thought process," he said. He spanked her then, and got the desired reaction. "Are you going to move in with me?"

"No," she said, still laughing.

He spanked her again. A little harder this time. "What did you say?"

She kicked her legs. "No, no, no, no, no!"

"You're a very bad girl," he told her.

She squirmed and slid off his lap. She stood up and pulled off the T-shirt. He looked at her, looked closely. She had lost more weight. He could see her ribs clearly through her skin. He had never really noticed it before, not like now.

"If you want me to move in, you have to catch me!" she said, and ran toward the bedroom.

He was close behind her.

On the bed, they were wrapped up in each other's limbs. He kissed the small of her neck. Ran his fingertips through her short black hair.

"I caught you!" he said. "Does that mean you're moving in?"

"I'll move in this weekend," she told him. "But you have to do something first."

"What?"

Her hand grabbed his crotch. "You have to move into *me*."

CHAPTER FIFTEEN

"Hello, Lash?" the voice on the phone said.

"Antony?" Lash answered, surprised. "We have an appointment next Tuesday, right?"

"Right-o!" he said. "But I was calling you about something else. I wanted to ask if you had a chance to think about that proposal I talked to you about the last time you were here."

"You mean about expanding my clientele?"

"That's the one," Antony said. "Have you thought about it?"

"A little," Lash said. "You see, I'm kind of in the middle of some changes right now, and things are hectic around here. Can I give you an answer when I see you on Tuesday?"

"Well," Antony said, then hesitated. "I was thinking maybe I could talk you into coming over tonight. It's a special occasion. I'm having a few close friends over, and I really want to give them a night to remember. And it will give you a chance to sell your talents, if you know what I mean."

"You want me to drop by for a couple of hours?"

"If you have other plans, I'll understand," Antony said. "I know this is short notice. We can always do it some other time, I guess."

"Well, I kind of did have other plans."

"Enough said. I totally understand. I'm sorry I didn't arrange all this beforehand, but it kind of came out of the blue. If you did consider it, though, I could guarantee a very attractive fee. I'll pay the regular amount per person, and then I'll even kick in a little bonus, for the inconvenience."

Lash thought about it. "I could always use the money," he said. Even though he hardly ever spent anything beyond rent and bills.

"You'll do it?"

"Can I get back to you about it?"

"Like I said, I'm making plans as we speak. It's happening real soon, and I really have to have an answer."

"Okay, I'll do it," Lash said. "What time do you want me to come over."

"How about around nine?"

"I'll be there."

"Sorry about disrupting your evening," Antony said. "I really owe you one."

Lash hung up the phone, noticing Miranda sitting over on the sofa, looking at him suspiciously.

"I have a job tonight," Lash said.

"Do you really have to go?" she asked. "There's a new movie I want to see tonight."

"I'll take you tomorrow," Lash said. "It'll still be there."

"I thought we had the night all to ourselves," Miranda said. "Who would call you on such short notice?"

"This guy named Antony," Lash said. "Me and him go way back. He offered me extra money, and I do have bills to pay, you know."

"What kind of work is it, anyway?" Miranda asked.

He still hadn't told her. She was moving in, and he still hadn't come clean about what he did for a living. *No more lies,* he told himself. *When she moves in, I'll tell her everything.*

"Just odds and ends," he told her.

"What does that mean?"

"I really should get dressed. I've been so lazy today."

"I wish you didn't have to go."

"Same here, but he doesn't ask me to drop by at night like this too often. It must be something special."

"Try and get back as fast as you can."

"Sure," Lash said. "I'll just get it over with and come right back. I promise."

She had come over a couple of hours before, and they had just finished dinner.

He went to the bathroom to change.

When he came out, she ran over to him.

"You look great," she said. "I wish you were dressing up for me."

He kissed her.

"I'll be waiting for you," she said.

"I know."

"Don't work too hard," she said. "I want you all to myself when you get back. And we have to move my stuff in the morning. I'm taking the day off work so we can get it done quicker."

"I know."

"You know a lot of things," she said.

"I know."

CHAPTER SIXTEEN

"I'm overjoyed that you could make it!" Antony said, ushering Lash into his penthouse apartment. A party had already begun inside. There were a few people there, talking and drinking champagne.

"Sure thing," Lash said. "As long as this doesn't become a habit."

"I knew you'd come through for me," Antony said. He led Lash into the kitchen, where they could be alone.

"I transferred your payment already," Antony said. "I figure it's better to do it beforehand. I can barely function afterward, as you know. When you're done, you can leave when you like."

"Thanks."

"Did everything go okay with the limo?"

"I was waiting outside when it came. No problem."

"Well, it's party time," Antony said. "Do you want anything to eat or drink before all the guests arrive?"

"No, thanks. I ate dinner already."

Antony led Lash back into the living room. A couple of people looked familiar. He recognized the model from the other day. She smiled at him.

"Have something to drink," Antony said. "Really, it will give you something to do while you wait."

"Okay," Lash said.

He walked over to the bar. A bartender took his order for a Tanqueray on the rocks. Lash went over to one corner and leaned against a wall, trying to blend in with the furniture. He really would have preferred not to be here. He never felt very comfortable at parties. Miranda always gave him a hard time about that. He looked around the room. More people were arriving.

Lash recognized a girl named Cindy, just coming in. She was an old girlfriend of Antony's. She had been Antony's partner in the first enhancement session Lash had done for him. She had been a tall, curvy blonde, but she had since become a redhead. Lash wondered if one of the other women in the room was the Essie who Antony had been talking about. Maybe he had given up on her completely, when she failed to show up earlier, and had moved on to someone else. Antony had a knack for moving on when he got bored.

The model from the other day walked over to where Lash was. He had been watching Cindy and hadn't noticed her approach.

"Funny running into you again," she said.

"Oh, hi," Lash said.

"My name is Joselyn," she said. "I don't know if Antony bothered to mention that."

"Mine's Lash."

"I know," she said. "That's an unusual name."

"My father liked to watch old westerns. I'm named after an old cowboy actor."

"Really?"

"Do you know what the big occasion is?"

"Antony comes up with these things on a whim," she said. "Whenever he's a little down, he throws a party to pick up his spirits."

"Attention!" Antony called out. He was standing in the middle of the room.

The buzz of voices continued.

"Attention, please!"

Everyone stopped talking and looked in his direction.

"I promised everyone something special tonight," Antony announced. "And I meant it. If you remember before, I've mentioned to all of you at certain times about someone I knew who could enhance certain sensations…some of you have even experienced it first-hand. Well, that gentleman is with us here tonight."

The people applauded. Some of them turned to look at Lash, who was still trying to blend in with the wall.

Cindy smiled and waved at him.

He waved back, feeling very self-conscious. But he had always found her to be very attractive. Lash envied Antony his lifestyle, sometimes.

"Well, if everyone is settled," Antony said. "Let the games begin!"

Joselyn turned to Lash. "God, imagine, twice in one week! I must really be high on Antony's list if he's sharing you with me this much."

Lash drained his glass and nodded.

"Well," she said. "I'll be seeing you."

She walked over to where Antony was, talking to some of the other guests.

Some of the people had begun undressing. In the middle of conversations, they removed articles of clothing. Doing little silly dances. Some people started making out with partners, deep kissing and fondling one another. Getting into the mood.

Lash stayed put and waited.

Cindy walked over to where he was. He was still impressed with how stunning she was.

"Long time no see," she said. "I really got off the last time we met. I'm just sorry it's been so long. It was like heaven or something. I just wanted to thank you."

"Just doing my job," Lash said, then smiled.

"When I heard that tonight would be more of the same, I jumped at the chance," she said. "Do you plan to take part in the festivities at all? Or are you going to keep your distance, like the old days?"

"I can't really join in if I'm going to do my thing."

"Oh," Cindy said. She looked into his eyes for a moment, trying to collect her thoughts. "Listen, I've always wanted to have another session with you, but, since we broke up, Antony has been really tight-assed about giving me your number. He wants to hog you all to himself."

Cindy handed him a slip of paper. "Here's my number. Give me a call sometime, and I'll make it worth your while. Antony isn't the only one with a rich daddy, and I'll pay you whatever he pays."

"I'll keep that in mind," Lash said, putting the piece of paper in his pocket.

"You do that," she said. "I think you're real talented. Well, I guess I'd better mingle. I wanted to thank you now for what you'll be doing. I'll be all jelly by the time you're through."

Cindy squeezed his arm and went to get friendly with some of her friends.

Antony came over when things seemed to be getting more intense.

"How are you feeling?" he asked Lash.

"Fine," Lash said.

"You get yourself another drink and I'll get everyone ready for your little performance."

Antony walked over to the doorway that led to a corridor. "Okay, everybody, follow me!"

People followed him. Kissing and groping all the way.

Lash went over to the bar. The bartender was gone. Someone must have snagged him into joining the party. Lash went behind the bar and poured himself a fresh glass of gin. He watched as the last people left the room.

He downed the drink.

He waited a few minutes for things to get organized.

Then he took off his clothes and folded them neatly. Put them on a chair.

Lash walked down the hallway to where the people were. It was dimly lit, but he couldn't miss the sounds or the scents.

The room was large. The furniture was missing, but there were lots of pillows everywhere. Everyone was stretched out on the carpet. They were kissing and fondling in earnest. Lash took his cue and got down on the carpet in area that had been cleared for him.

He stretched out. The lush carpeting felt nice against his bare back.

Lash closed his eyes and gently started rocking side to side.

Slowly at first, then gaining momentum.

Not long after he began, he heard heightened sounds of pleasure. It began with small cries from some of the women.

Then some men piped in. It was like a chorus. Each section adding their part.

The sounds were like a complex musical composition. And he was the conductor.

He listened until it all became part of his trance.

In the trance, he was in a kind of a half-life. Every once in a while, he could feel someone grope for him, trying to pull him into the action. But he resisted. Eventually, they would give up and get lost in the sensations.

He kept rolling.

When he came out of the trance, he opened his eyes and stared up at the ceiling. It was almost like coming out of anesthesia after an operation. Or coming down after a particularly vivid drug trip.

The room was quieter now. There were sounds here and there, but mostly there was loud breathing.

Lash stood up. Leaving the room, he looked back briefly. But it didn't look like a room full of people. It looked like a conglomeration of fleshy body parts.

Lash found the bathroom and took a shower. He really didn't want to go back to Miranda all sweaty, and he knew that Antony wouldn't mind. He scrubbed himself and then he went and got his clothes.

He got dressed in the living room. He was completely alone. No one had even attempted to stir from the orgy room.

Glasses half-filled with champagne were everywhere around the room. Crumbs of food were ground into the carpet.

He knew that his limousine would be waiting downstairs. He put on his jacket and pressed the button for the elevator.

In the other room, people were starting to stir.

The elevator door opened. Lash got in, feeling like he had actually accomplished something tonight.

CHAPTER SEVENTEEN

Miranda's things were moved in, or at least those things there was room for. Which wasn't much. Her furniture and half her wardrobe had to stay in her old apartment, which she would continue to pay rent for, until they decided what to do. The plan was, if the arrangement worked out, they'd eventually start looking for a bigger place.

"This is going to be neat," Miranda said. "It's like a new adventure."

"You bet," Lash said, feeling genuinely happy.

The phone rang.

Lash was going to let the answering machine pick it up, but he was afraid it might be Lizzie, calling to bother him, and he didn't want Miranda to hear it. He didn't want to ruin the moment. So he picked it up.

"Hello?"

"Lash, is that you?" a female voice said on the other end. He didn't recognize it immediately. "It's Cindy, from last night."

"Hi!"

"I know I was supposed to wait for you to call me, but I wormed your number out of Antony, and I just couldn't wait. Not after what happened last night. It was incredible. I was wondering if we could make an appointment for some time this week."

"Well…"

"This isn't a bad time to call, is it?" Cindy asked. When he hesitated, she said, "I'm not being too pushy, am I?"

"No, not at all," he assured her. "I just don't know what my schedule will be like this week, that's all."

"Why don't we make an appointment for Thursday at noon,"

she suggested. "If you have to change it later, I'll understand. You still have my number, don't you?"

"Yeah," he said.

"So what do you think?" she asked, sounding a little anxious.

"That sounds okay."

"Great," she said. "I live at 223 Oak Haven Place. Just take the elevator all the way up."

He wrote it down on a pad by the phone.

"Got it."

"You don't know how much I appreciate this," she told him. "You're a darling. And I really want to thank you for last night. It was stupendous."

He laughed, nervously. "Yeah, sure."

"Well, see you then," she said.

They both hung up.

"Who was that?" Miranda asked.

"A new client," he said. "The money will help when we decide to move."

"Can't they just let you enjoy your weekend in peace?" Miranda asked, looking disappointed.

"The appointment is for later in the week," he said. "The rest of the weekend belongs to us."

"I'm glad," Miranda said.

He grabbed her and held her close. They kissed.

"You're the only thing on my mind for the next two days."

"I have an idea," she said. "Let's pretend like it's our honeymoon. We're all done moving for now, so let's spend the rest of the time in bed."

"Sounds good to me," Lash said. "But what about food? I'm starving!"

"Can't we order something that can be delivered?" Miranda asked. "We can pretend like it's room service."

"I have a few take-out menus here," he said, rifling through some papers near the phone. "How about Chinese food?"

"Fine," she said. "I'm not very hungry, anyway."

"I'll order the usual stuff," he said, punching out the number on the phone.

As he placed the order, Miranda began to undress in front of him, doing a seductive striptease.

When he got off the phone, he said, "Aren't you going to wait until we eat first?"

"How about a quickie?" she said. "They won't get here for at least half an hour. And I want you now."

Lash didn't argue.

She took his hand and led him to the bedroom.

He was going to like this.

CHAPTER EIGHTEEN

Not long after they'd finished eating, Miranda went to the bathroom.

Lash sat on the couch, rereading the little slips of paper that had come in their fortune cookies.

As he read, he could hear faint, strange sounds coming from the bathroom. At first, he thought they were coming from the television. But they weren't. He quietly got up from the couch and walked over. He put his ear to the door.

Miranda was throwing up.

He resisted the urge to knock and ask if she was okay.

Instead, he just listened.

It aroused him.

CHAPTER NINETEEN

B ZZZZZZZ!
     Miranda jerked upright in bed and turned to look at Lash. He was sound asleep, unaffected. Ear plugs saw to that. She grabbed the clock and turned it over. It vibrated in her hands as she searched, bleary-eyed, for the button to shut it off. She finally found the button, pressed it.

It stopped.

It was Lash's clock, but he rarely used it. He didn't have regular hours, like she did.

He rolled over. Kept moving until he was sleeping on his stomach.

She leaned over and looked at his back.

On his left shoulder blade was a tattoo, finely detailed, of a fly. It was almost the size of an old 45 record. On his right shoulder blade there was a slightly larger tattoo of a black widow spider.

She gently touched the spider, tracing its outline with her fingertips.

Lash did not stir.

She had seen the tattoos countless times, but they still intrigued her.

Miranda leaned over and kissed him between the shoulder blades. Then she got out of bed.

She toyed with the idea of calling in sick and prolonging their first weekend together, but she wasn't sure what his plans were for the day, and she had already taken a day off on Friday to move. Besides, it might be a good idea to establish a routine right off the bat.

There was a chair by the window. She sat down on it,

watching him sleep again. He was so still and quiet. Not a snore, not a sound. She had never known anyone who slept so peacefully.

He had gained some weight since they first met.

His blonde hair was longer than hers. His arms seemed thinner than they should have been, but they were muscular.

Miranda rubbed her eyes. Then she got her clothes together and went to the bathroom to take a shower.

While she was showering, he woke up and took out his ear plugs. He went out into the living room and turned on the television. An old gangster movie was on.

He watched until a commercial came on, then he went into the kitchen and made coffee for both of them. Neither one of them ate breakfast very often.

When she was dressed, Miranda came out into the living room and was surprised to find Lash awake.

"There's coffee brewing," he told her.

She kissed him and then went to get herself a cup.

He went to the bathroom to empty his bladder.

Not much later, she kissed him good-bye at the door, and left for work.

Lash went back to bed.

When Lash got up a second time and got dressed himself, he looked around the apartment. It was like a different place, now that Miranda had moved in.

He looked at the clothes in the half of the bedroom closet that was now hers. At her underwear in the drawers that were now hers. He went into the bathroom and opened the medicine cabinet and the small, shallow closet that was used for storing towels and sheets. In these he found bottles. Laxatives and vitamin pills, and strange prescription drugs he had never heard of.

Lash lifted the toilet seat to urinate. He noticed a small spot of dried vomit on the inside of the rim.

He fantasized about Miranda, naked, bent over the toilet, vomiting.

He felt a shiver go through him.

CHAPTER TWENTY

"You were a real hit at the party," Antony said. "I really want to thank you for showing up."

"Sure," Lash said. "Thanks for the bonus."

"You earned it."

The apartment was mostly empty. All the furniture that had been in the living room was now gone.

"Are you moving out?" Lash asked, standing over at the window.

"Yeah," Antony said. "I need a bigger pad. Do you like this place?"

"I could never afford it."

"Even with your income from your other clients?"

"It takes a lot out of me," Lash said. "There's a limit to how often I can do it."

"This place would be perfect for you," Antony said. "Maybe we could work something out. I could deduct money from your rent, for your services."

"Don't go to any trouble for me," Lash said. "I'm really not interested in moving here, and I don't need any favors. I don't want to be your kept man."

"So touchy!" Antony said, and smiled. "I haven't seen this side of you for a while. I kind of missed it."

Lash pretended to enjoy the view. He stood at the window, looking out over the brightly lit city.

"Listen, you wouldn't be a kept man. And you wouldn't be in my debt or anything. It wouldn't be like a loan or anything. I'd just sublet it to you, that's all. And if I do that, I could charge whatever I want."

"I don't know," Lash said. "I'd still feel like I owed you

something. I'm not too crazy about feeling that way."

"You still want to maintain that distance, huh?"

"As much as I can," Lash said. "Although, with you, I've kind of broken that rule already."

"What's wrong with being friends?"

"I have other clients, is all," Lash said. "It's a business thing."

Lash finished his gin.

"Let me refill that," Antony said, taking the glass from him.

"We go a long way, you and me," Antony said. The bar was gone, but he had a couple of bottles on the floor and a bucket of ice. One was gin, because that was what Lash mostly drank. The other was scotch. Antony refilled his own glass, too.

The oldest. Lash thought back to the first time they'd met. He was married to Lizzie then, and she had arranged it.

It was her idea to use his talent for money.

"So where are you moving to?" Lash asked, as Antony handed him the glass.

"My family has a house out on the island. They never use it. It's right on the water. Big, spacious. Beautiful. It seemed a waste to have it there, unoccupied. So I figured I'd take it over. Besides, this place has gotten too small for the kind of get-togethers I want to arrange."

"So we'll still have our sessions."

"Of course," Antony said. "I have no intention of giving that up."

They both looked out the window.

"Look, as soon as I'm moved in and settled, I'll give you a call and arrange things. I'll send a car to collect you."

They were just killing time until Antony's date arrived.

"So what do you do with your time off, Lash?"

"Not much," Lash said. "I go to the gym and work out a lot."

"You look to be in pretty good shape."

"I try."

"How's Lizzie?"

"I don't really see her much anymore," Lash said. "Since the divorce."

"Oh, yeah," Antony said. "I forgot. Sorry."

"It's okay."

"It's just that we don't talk about her very much. So I forgot."

"It's okay, really."

"So are you seeing anyone new these days?"

"Yeah," Lash said. "In fact, she just moved in with me."

"Really?" Antony said. He seemed amazed. "This is not like you, opening up like this. Usually you keep your answers short and sweet. So, what's her name?"

"Miranda," Lash said.

"What's she like?"

"She makes me happy," Lash said, at the same time wondering how much longer it would be before he got bored and wanted to move on. He had been thinking about that a lot since Miranda moved in.

"I'm glad to hear it," Antony said. "Usually you're all business. I like seeing this other side of you. You should show it more often."

Lash drained his glass.

There were chimes and Antony's private elevator opened.

It was a new girl. Brunette. Looked to be in her early twenties. Maybe even nineteen. Something about her eyes reminded him of Lizzie.

And she seemed more than a little wired.

She had probably been sent by an escort service. The ones he didn't recognize usually were.

"Would you like something to drink?" Antony asked.

"Sure," the girl said. She looked at Lash. "Is it going to be the three of us?" she asked. "Because I was told it was just you."

"Don't worry about it," Antony said.

She laughed nervously. "What does he do, just watch or something?"

"You'll see. It will be a pleasant surprise. I promise you."

She laughed again. It was forced.

Antony poured her a drink. She drank it too quickly.

"Relax, dear," Antony said. "We're all friends here. Tell you what, we'll go into the bedroom and get acquainted. Then my friend will join us a little later."

She was going to complain again about the threesome, but

Antony put a finger to her lips to shush her. He led her down the corridor to the bedroom.

They closed the door.

Lash looked at his watch, then went over and poured himself another drink.

He was starting to feel a little drunk.

CHAPTER TWENTY-ONE

Thursday. Late morning.

When he got there, Lash noticed that he was a little more nervous than usual. He had been thinking about it on the way up, and he had to admit to himself that it had to be, in this case, because he was genuinely attracted to his client.

He got out of the bright white elevator and walked down a lushly carpeted hallway. The carpeting and walls were also white. He came to a large room. Cindy smiled when she saw him.

"It's great to see you," she said. "And you're right on time."

She was wrapped in a velvety robe. Obviously, she had just gotten out of the shower. Her hair was wrapped in a towel.

"Did you have any trouble finding the place?" she asked him.

"No, not at all."

There was an awkward silence. He looked around the apartment at the variety of vases and little statuettes, and the colorful paintings of landscapes that adorned the walls.

He could tell she loved beautiful things.

He felt like he didn't belong here.

"Would you care for a drink?" she asked him.

"No, thanks," he said. He had been drinking a lot lately and needed to cut down.

He sat on a chair that looked like an antique, and almost got back up again. He was afraid it was fragile, but it turned out to be quite sturdy. She sat across from him, on a loveseat. As she sat down, her robe fell open, revealing the fact that she had recently had a bikini wax. She did not make an attempt to cover up. In fact, she pretended not to notice.

"So how does this usually work?" she asked him. "Do I pay before or after?"

"It doesn't really matter," he said, trying not to look at her too obviously. "I guess most people pay beforehand."

"We already discussed your fee on the phone," she said. "So I already have it ready for you." She fished in the left-hand pocket of her robe. She extracted an envelope. She leaned forward, handing it to him.

She fumbled with her robe, closing it again, and fidgeted in her seat.

"So, is there anything we have to do to prepare?" she asked him.

"Not really," he said. "I'm ready whenever you are. Is there going to be anyone else?"

"No," she said. "Just you and me. Since this is the first time you've come here, I wanted to keep it simple. Would you like to get more comfortable?"

He poured himself a drink after all. When he finished it, he put the glass down and stood up.

"Where do you want to…"

"Follow me," she said, taking his hand.

She led him up three steps and down a hallway. They stopped in front of a closed door. She turned to look at him, then she opened the door.

It was a bedroom. In one corner was a large, circular bed. The rest of the room was devoid of furniture.

"I know you need space for what you do," she told him.

She walked over to the bed and threw herself down on it. There were various sex toys beside her.

Lash got undressed. He put them in a neat pile in one corner of the room. He was already aroused, and it made him more nervous. He wasn't used to being the center of attention like this.

He got down on the floor, with his back to her.

"When do you want me to begin?" he asked.

"Wait a minute," she said. He could hear her moving around on the bed, taking her robe off.

He wanted so badly to turn around and look at her. *Watch her.*

"You can turn around," she said.

"It really works best if I do it this way," he said, his back still to her as he sat on the carpet.

"Don't start yet," she said. "But you can turn around."

Part of him wanted to keep all this professional. But another part wanted to join her. He hesitated.

"Please turn around."

Slowly, he crawled so that he was facing her.

She began a performance that was clearly for his benefit.

She spread her legs, and slowly ran a finger from her navel to her shaved pubis. Her fingers caressed her vagina. One finger inserted itself within. Then another.

He sat there, watching, and she watched him in turn, through slitted eyes.

The sheets were disheveled beneath her, around her. She reached beneath the sheets with a free hand and pulled out a long, red vibrator.

She switched it on and it began to hum.

"Start rolling," she said softly.

At first, the words didn't register. He was mesmerized by her. She opened her eyes wider and smiled, inserting the tip of the vibrator into her moist vagina. She made a low, groany noise. Then she pulled the vibrator away.

"Ahh," she breathed. "Please start rolling."

This time, the words registered. He reluctantly got down on the floor and began to roll back and forth. Side to side. He started off slow, and then gradually gathered momentum.

He continued to hear her noises when he slipped into his trance state. Usually, in this state, he could distance himself from his environment. He could get lost in his own thoughts and mental imagery. But her sounds chased after him, refusing to let him escape completely.

When he stopped rolling, he lay on the floor, breathing hard.

He saw that he had ejaculated while in the trance. This hadn't happened to him in a long time. He was soaked with sweat, and too tired to care.

She had stopped making loud noises, but he could hear her breathing.

He tried not to make a sound, as he stayed on his back.

"Lash," she called out to him, in a soft voice.

He did not answer her.

"Lash," she called out again, a little louder this time. "Come here."

He slowly raised himself up on his elbows. He turned and looked at the bed.

She was stretched out. Her feet dangled over the edge. He could not see her face.

"Wow," she said hoarsely.

He knew she would be spent; she would probably be drifting off to sleep soon. He felt pretty exhausted himself, like he had just run a marathon. She didn't say anything else and he closed his eyes.

When he woke up an hour later, Cindy was stretched out on the carpet beside him, waiting for him.

They made love.

Lash was in the shower when he faintly heard his cell phone ringing. It couldn't be anything urgent. *Let it go to voicemail.*

He took his time drying off and then checked his messages. It was Antony.

"Do you remember what I said about moving, and that I'd arrange to have you come out to the new place? Well, I've been thinking. I still have the penthouse for as long as I want it, and now it has no furniture, so there's lots of space. It makes sense to just keep meeting there. That is, if you're really sure that you're not interested in it yourself. How about we make our next appointment for Tuesday, as always? Call me back if there's a problem."

Lash thought that was the end of the message, then Antony started talking again.

"Oh, by the way, I hope you don't mind, but I gave Cindy your number. She kind of wormed it out of me. I know I should have asked you first. I don't think she'll be any trouble."

CHAPTER TWENTY-TWO

Lizzie took a bite of a tuna salad on rye sandwich. She washed it down with bourbon. On the kitchen wall, there were photos of Lash. Pictures of when the two of them were younger and happy. When they were in love. When things were much more clear-cut than they were now. *When she didn't have to feel ashamed for needing him.*

On the table, near her, was a copy of his apartment key.

She grabbed the key and fondled it in her hand. It was cool and real, and she squeezed her hand tightly around it.

Lizzie had tried to get her mind off him. She had tried to work extra hours and lose herself in her job. But the company was cutting down on employee overtime, and, to tell the truth, she really hated being there anyway. It just reinforced how empty her life was. And it didn't take her mind off Lash. Not by a long shot. Even at her job, she had a small, framed photograph of him on her desk. If anyone asked, she told them they were still married, but going through a rough patch. Everything would be all right.

She hadn't dated anyone in months. Not a *real* date. A few times she let men pick her up at bars and they'd end up fucking. But it was so hollow, so empty, that it made things worse. Things like that just reinforced how badly she wanted Lash.

But he didn't want her. *That was clear.*

Feeling the key in her hand, she knew that if she ever actually used it, it would just create more trouble between them. But she also knew that, eventually, she would have to see him again. Somehow.

CHAPTER TWENTY-THREE

L ash woke in the middle of the night, to find himself alone in bed.

The glowing face of the alarm clock showed that it was close to two in the morning.

He got out of bed and went out into the hall. The bathroom door was closed. Instead of checking it out, he went to the kitchen, trying to be as quiet as possible.

In the kitchen, the condition of the dining table revealed that someone had been eating. The container he had put the leftover curry in was empty, as well as a quart carton of ice cream.

He walked back to the bathroom. He didn't have to put his ear to the door. The sounds were clear. Miranda was vomiting again.

This time, he was not satisfied just to stand outside the door and listen. He turned the knob. The door was unlocked.

She was on the floor, dressed only in a sheer nightgown, bent over the toilet bowl, oblivious to his entrance.

Watching her, he found himself getting incredibly aroused. A silent observer, overcome with passion.

He removed his briefs and got down on the floor behind her. She had stopped vomiting for the moment, and he tried to mount her.

"Get the fuck away from me!" she cried out, pushing him away. She did not look at him.

She began heaving again.

He sat on the floor, leaning against the wall, watching her. Aware of his erection, as he watched her body quivering while she threw up her late-night feast.

Once she started vomiting again, she seemed to have forgotten about him, but he didn't mind.

He jerked himself off as he watched her.

CHAPTER TWENTY-FOUR

L ash got to Antony's apartment on time for their appointment. The limousine didn't show up, so he got a taxi.

The doorman called up to Antony's room, but didn't get an answer.

"I know he's up there," the doorman said. "He went up a few hours ago, when I started my shift."

"We have an appointment," Lash said.

"I recognize you," the doorman said. "You come here every week. Maybe he's just busy. Just go on up."

"Thanks," Lash said and went to where the private elevator was.

He rode up.

The elevator opened when it reached the penthouse.

The big living room was bare of furniture, like the last time he had been there, but now there was an aluminum ladder, on its side, in the middle of the floor.

It looked as if the ladder had been knocked over.

Lash stepped out of the elevator. *It was then that he saw Antony.*

Antony had affixed some kind of hook to the high ceiling. And, attached to the hook was a noose. Antony was *hanging from it*. His face had a bluish tinge. His tongue was protruding and his eyes were bulging. The ladder had obviously been his way up.

Lash looked up at the corpse that had been Antony. Then down at a puddle that had formed beneath him, on the carpet. His body had evacuated in death.

Standing there, Lash felt a loud ringing in his ears. It got progressively louder. Then, there was an electricity in the air that crackled around him. It increased, making his hair stand on end.

His fingertips tingled, and then the tingling became painful.

The next thing he knew, Lash was down on the carpet, rolling back and forth. He found himself entering a trance, even though he tried to stop himself. He had lost control of himself, as if he had ceased being a man and had become a kind of tool. Even when he was at the peak of the whole *enhancement thing* in the past, it never felt like this.

The trance got deeper, and then his consciousness pulled away altogether, letting the trance take over completely.

All his senses closed down, and everything blinked into darkness.

When he came out of the trance, he felt disoriented.

He was lying on the carpet. He could make out the shape of Antony, still hanging from the ceiling above him.

Lash was covered in sweat and breathing hard. He wiped his face with his hands and sat up.

He had no idea how long the trance had lasted.

He got to his feet. There was a phone attached to the wall. He stumbled toward it and grabbed the receiver, put it to his ear. On the wall, the phone's buttons glowed in the dark. He pressed 9-1-1.

"Give me the police," he said, when he got an answer.

Lash reported Antony's death and hung up the phone. Then he went to the elevator and pressed the button to go down.

He could have tried to get away, but the doorman saw him go up. Besides, a coroner would be able to determine the cause of death, and whether it was a suicide.

Lash tried to calm himself. *I'll just say I passed out. Which I did.*

The elevator opened.

He got inside.

He did not look at Antony again as the doors closed.

If I stay any longer, I might start rolling again, he thought.

He held his breath the whole way down.

When the elevator doors opened, he went over to the doorman.

"Mr. Chester," Lash said to the man. "He's dead. I called the police."

"Dead," the man asked. "What do you mean?"

"He hung himself," Lash said. "When I saw him, I just passed out. I don't know how long I was up there."

He must have looked disoriented. Still, the doorman seemed genuinely concerned. The man looked at his watch. "You went up there about an hour ago. So, are the police on their way?"

"Yes, yes," Lash said, feeling delirious.

"Maybe you should stay."

"I will. I just need some air."

Lash kept walking until he was outside. He took a deep breath of the night air and then just stood there. There was no use in running. He might as well get this over with.

He could hear a siren approaching.

CHAPTER TWENTY-FIVE

L ash refused to get out of bed. He had been sleeping the whole day. More precisely, he had been existing in a kind of middle state between sleep and wakefulness. When she got back from work, Miranda found him still in bed.

When he had come back the night before, he told her what had happened at Antony's place. He told her he had had some kind of seizure when he discovered the body, and it scared the hell out of him. And he told her about his talk with the police.

"I rolled around on the carpet against my will," he said. "I had no control over it."

"But you're okay now."

"No," he said. "Something happened to me, rolling around on the floor in the same room with his corpse like that. I feel like I sucked in some of the death that was in that room. Even now, I feel filled with death."

"That doesn't make any sense," she told him. "You have to fight this. You have to resist giving in to this whole thing. If you don't fight this, it will destroy you."

"I can feel it inside me," he said, not listening to her. "Pure death!"

"No," she told him. "You're alive. You can breathe, you can talk to me."

"But I feel it inside me. Paralyzing me."

"You have to eat something," she said.

Eventually, she left him alone.

When Miranda came back, he was still there, huddled in a ball on his side of the bed. He hadn't moved more than a few inches the whole day.

She got in beside him and turned off the light.

Miranda put her arms around him. He was very stiff. Almost like a corpse himself.

The next day, Lash got up early and fixed a big breakfast. He felt like himself again.

"God, it's good to see you back to normal," Miranda said, when she got up.

"Help yourself," he said. "There's plenty."

She drank coffee and watched him eat. "I don't eat breakfast, remember? Besides, I'm not hungry."

"When I woke up, I was starving."

"You didn't eat all day yesterday," she said. "It's no wonder."

She got up and got ready for work.

"Do you want me to stay home with you today?" she asked.

"No," he said. "Don't change your plans for me. Besides, I have a lot to do today."

"You're not going to work today, are you?" she asked.

"Don't worry about it," he said. "Go to work Everything is back to normal now."

Reluctantly, realizing that she couldn't win, Miranda kissed him, then left.

He continued to eat.

His cell rang. It was Cindy.

"Did you hear about Antony?" she asked.

"Yeah," he said. "I was there. I'm the one who found him."

"That's awful," she said. "How are you holding up?"

"I'm okay," he said.

"I knew he was feeling down lately," Cindy said. "I knew he had a lot of things on his mind. But I didn't know it was *that* bad. Are you going to the funeral on Saturday?"

"No," he said.

"Oh," she said. "It's just that I was thinking of going, and I was wondering if you'd go with me."

"No," Lash said. "I don't handle that stuff very well."

"Do you still want to get together today? Are you up to it?"

"To tell the truth," he said. "I kind of forgot about that. I guess the stuff with Antony did shake me up a little."

Then, "I guess I'm glad you called."

"You want to postpone our appointment?" she asked.

"It might be for the best."

"I guess I really should go to the wake today," she said. "How about we postpone it until after the funeral?" Cindy asked.

"Sounds good," he said.

"See you next week," she said. "And Lash?"

"Yeah?"

"You've got my number; give me a call if you ever need someone to talk to."

"Sure," he told her.

She hung up. He waited a few minutes, then he hung up, too.

He went back to the dining table and finished eating. He had made eggs and bacon and sausages and toast. What he didn't already have in the house, he had gone out and gotten at a convenience store that was open twenty-four hours a day, two blocks away. It was a good sign that he was eating, that he had gone outside.

He poured a shot of bourbon and chased it with some orange juice.

When he was done eating, he sat there for a few minutes, wondering what the hell to do.

CHAPTER TWENTY-SIX

Later that morning, Lash went out again to the liquor store. While he was looking in the beer cooler, someone came up behind him and put a hand on his shoulder.

"Fancy bumping into you here."

He turned around quickly. He had no idea who it could be. He was surprised when he saw the face smiling back at him.

"Hi, Lash."

"Joselyn," he said. "Good to see you."

She was wearing a very tight dress that accentuated her curves and a light jacket. And she was so close to him. He found it hard to breathe for a second.

"That was awful news about Antony," she said, and the smile disappeared. "Are you going to his wake later?"

"I don't think so," Lash said. "I didn't really know him that well. And I'm not really good at those kinds of things."

"Sorry to hear it," she said. "I was hoping to see some friendly faces there. I'll tell you, I have no idea who's going to show up to that thing. It could be kind of a freak show."

He must have looked confused, because she smiled again. "He had some very strange friends. You probably never met them. Or if you did, you didn't talk to them enough to find out how weird they are."

"I guess so."

"Is it true you're the one who found him? Dead, I mean."

"Yeah," Lash said. "It was a pretty bad scene."

"I would think so," she said. "Must have been awful for you."

"He was a good guy," Lash said. "And it was a real shock to see him like that."

"Yes," she looked over his shoulder, at the cooler. "Getting some beer?"

"Yeah, just some odds and ends."

"You know, Lash," she said. The way she smiled now seemed to tell him that she knew he had always been attracted to her. That it was a private secret between them. "I'd always wanted to hire you for some other jobs. You know, aside from Antony's things. But he was very protective of your phone number. He always made a big deal about having to ask you first before he gave it to anyone."

"Yeah, Antony was really good about that."

"Oh, I'm sure he was. I know he considered you quite a find and wasn't eager to share you too much."

"I don't know if I'd put it that way."

"I know this isn't exactly a good time," Joselyn said. "But I really would like to hire you, like I said. I mean, you really blew my mind, you know. And now that poor Antony is gone, you'll probably need other clients."

"Yeah, I guess so."

"Here," she said, reaching into her purse. "I know all this must have really shaken you up. So take some time; you don't have to call me right away." She handed him her card. "But when you're up to it, give me a call. I really do want to see you again. And I'll pay you even more than Antony did."

He took the card and looked it over. But he really didn't see it. His senses were still focused on her, standing in front of him. "Okay."

"So I'll be hearing from you?" Joselyn said. "You promise?"

"Yeah, I'll call you sometime next week."

"*Early* next week, I hope. After the funeral on Sunday, I'm really going to need a pick-me-up."

"Early next week," he assured her.

"That's great," she said. "I'm so glad I bumped into you. It's great to see you again."

"Yeah, me too."

"Well, I better be going. Don't lose that card, okay?"

She looked like she was considering leaning forward and kissing him, but she stepped back instead. He could see a mischievous kind of twinkle in her eyes as she walked toward the counter.

"I'll look forward to next time," she said over her shoulder as she walked away.

He was a little shocked to see her there. Why would she be shopping in *this* neighborhood?

Lash picked out a couple of six-packs and headed to the register.

Joselyn was nowhere in sight.

CHAPTER TWENTY-SEVEN

When Lash got back to his apartment, he found he had a visitor. Lizzie was in the bedroom, naked and in the bed, waiting for his return.

"Are you crazy?" he asked her. "I told you that Miranda moved in with me, right? What if she came back instead of me, and found you like this?"

"I've been keeping track of your routines; I knew she would be at work."

"So you're stalking us now?" he asked, but the word "now" in this context seemed silly. She had been stalking him for a long time.

"Come to bed. Let's have a booty call."

"You've been drinking," Lash said. "Get out of here, right now."

"Come on, lover," Lizzie said. "Just give me a little taste. It's been so long, and I've got an itch I can't scratch."

"You better be dressed when I get back," he said. He went back out to the living room and put the six-packs down on the coffee table and tore one of the cans off the pack. He cracked it open and gulped it down.

Then he went back into the bedroom. Lizzie was still naked and waiting for him.

"I'm not going anywhere," she said.

She doesn't believe I'm serious about this, Lash thought. But then again, seeing her here like this, spread-eagle on the bed, he could not deny that he was tempted. Things weren't going quite as exciting as he had hoped for since Miranda moved in, and this was a nice distraction.

"You never take me seriously," he said.

"Because I know what you really want."

He began to take his clothes off and she smiled.

He was upon her before she knew what was happening. His hands were around her throat, holding her tightly, and his knees spread her legs apart farther. He pushed himself inside of her as he cut off her air supply. Her eyes were wide and staring up into his.

Lash wondered if she really believed that she could die right now.

He resisted the urge to punch her in the ribs. He really wanted to hurt her. To make her scream in pain. But somehow, he was able to keep himself in check and not let things go too far. He forced himself to let go right about when he thought things might get dangerous, and there were hand marks on her neck. She gasped for air, and then the breathing took on the sounds of orgasm.

He watched her writhe beneath him and then his climax began as well.

When he was spent, he pushed himself off her and rolled over on to his side.

She groaned, trying to catch her breath again. "You could have killed me," she said.

He did not respond.

She sat up, forcing herself to breathe and said, "I knew you couldn't resist."

He turned and she was holding her neck; her eyes were wet and a tear ran down one cheek, but she did not look upset. She had clearly enjoyed it.

"Now for dessert," she said, reaching for her purse beside the bed. She had her vibrator out before he could say a word and looked up at him expectantly.

Aw, what the hell, he thought, and climbed down onto the carpet at the foot of the bed.

He closed his eyes and started to roll back and forth. He could hear her breathing getting hard again above him. It was only a matter of time before she would start getting vocal. She wasn't one to keep quiet when she was enjoying herself.

As he entered the trance, all he could think was, *I have to get her out of here as soon as I can.*

CHAPTER TWENTY-EIGHT

L ash got out of the taxi, as it came to a stop outside the motel. He walked around until he found room forty-three. It was in the back of the building. There weren't any cars parked in the lot back there. He could not see inside the room. The curtains were closed.

Loose gravel crunched beneath his shoes as he walked.

Lash took a deep breath and knocked.

"Come in," a man's voice said. It was the voice of someone who was used to giving orders. A booming, powerful voice.

Lash went inside.

The room had been arranged to make things easier. The bed was pushed to one corner. The rest of the furniture was all pushed in another corner. The bathroom door was closed. His clients usually didn't take long to catch on and know how to prepare for his visits.

Mr. Gamble, who had to be about six foot four, was wearing a black mask that covered most of his face. He had a dark blue bathrobe on.

"It's good to see you again," he said. His booming voice had a slight Southern twang. "Thanks for coming on such short notice."

Lash had never seen the man without his mask. He didn't even know for sure if Gamble was his name. This was the fifth time Lash had ever seen him. The first time they met, the man had explained he was from out of town. He was only in the city a few times a year. But he had heard of Lash from a mutual friend. He never said who, but Lash always assumed Lizzie had had something to do with it. Now, he wasn't so sure.

There was a time when Lash had many clients. When he

would visit people almost every day. Back when he was with Lizzie. Many of the people were her contacts. Then he was sick for a while and cut way back on his client list. It had never gotten back to the volume of the old days. Lash was convinced it just took too much out of him. Lizzie had said back then that he just lacked ambition.

The man had had prostitutes with him the other times. One time, he had three girls with him.

There was a dim bulb in a light fixture over the bed. Lash looked at the man's mask. It looked like plastic or fabric around the eyes, and then a black veil hung below that, covering his nose and mouth. If he really wanted to, Lash thought could find out the man's identity. But he had no desire to do so. It didn't matter who he was.

Lash suspected that he was an important, powerful person. He saw it in the way the man carried himself. Even in the way he chose to disguise his identity. Trying to protect his reputation. Maybe, once, he had been caught in the act and was now extra careful.

"Let's get this done first," the man said, handing Lash an envelope. It was a cool day, and Lash put it in his coat pocket.

"Okay, honey, you can come out now."

The bathroom door opened. Out came a girl with long, peroxide-blonde hair. She was also wearing a mask. It was a pink mask, similar to the one the man wore. It made Lash think of a harem girl. She was wearing a bathrobe, too. Lavender. The robe was big on her, and Lash could tell both robes probably belonged to the man, because they both had the same initials on the right-hand pocket. KXB.

Lash stood where he was. Despite their preparations, there wasn't much room to move around.

"Is this him?" the girl asked. She had a nasal voice, and she sounded young.

"Yeah, that's him," the man said.

The way they stood there, with their masks. It was like Lash was in the bedroom of two superheroes. *Corporate Man and his trusty sidekick Peroxide Girl.*

"How come he isn't wearing a mask like us, honey?"

"I don't know," Corporate Man said. "I never asked him to. There's not much point to it now, is there?" He looked over at Lash. "You want a mask? I got another one if you want."

"No, thanks."

"Is he going to *watch* us?" Peroxide Girl asked.

"Naw, he ain't a peeper," Corporate Man said.

"I won't be watching," Lash assured her. "That's not why I'm here."

"Oh," Peroxide Girl said, sounding disappointed.

"Believe me, Sweety," Corporate Man said, sounding like God himself, with that big, booming voice. "Once we get started, you won't even know he's here. You won't even care."

That voice. Lash knew if he ever heard it outside this environment, there was no way he could mistake it. It etched itself in his mind.

"Is he going to do it *with* us?" Peroxide Girl asked.

"Naw, it ain't a threesome, honey."

"Is he going to film us?"

"Nothing like that, baby. I'd explain it, but it's too hard to explain. But, believe me, you'll like it."

"Are you sure?"

"Would I lie to you, babycakes?"

"I guess not."

Lash just stood there, watching them talk. It was better than TV.

"You want a drink?" Corporate Man asked Lash. "I've got some real smooth scotch."

"No, thanks," Lash said. "Maybe afterward."

"Suit yourself."

"I've got some wine," Peroxide Girl said. "You want any of that?"

"No, thanks."

"He's cute," Peroxide Girl said. "You sure he won't join in."

"That's not how it works," Corporate Man said, getting a little impatient. He turned to Lash. "Want to begin?"

"Any time you're ready," Lash said.

"Come on then, sweet cheeks," Corporate Man said and took Peroxide Girl by the hand and led her to the bed.

Lash got undressed. He never really thought about it before, but he didn't really need to get undressed along with them. Somehow, he had gotten into the habit anyway. Probably because being naked did seem to be a little less restrictive when he was rolling, and it probably put his clients at ease.

It was no big deal.

He could see them out of the corner of his eye. They had removed their robes and were fondling each other on the bed. Peroxide Girl was looking in his direction, checking out his body, still wondering what he was there for, if he wasn't joining in.

Lash got down on the floor. He lay there, waiting.

"Hey, mister, why don't you come over here with us," Peroxide Girl said. "There's plenty of room."

"Will you forget about him!" Corporate Man boomed.

Lash waited. He could hear their noises, soft and playful at first, and he could smell their scents. He waited until it sounded as if they had forgotten about him, and then Lash began to roll.

Slowly at first. Then, gradually building momentum.

The couple in bed could feel what was happening. Their noises got louder. The bed squeaked louder.

Lash went into his trance.

When he came out of it, it was over an hour later according to his watch, and the noises were still loud.

He continued to roll, but it was slower.

The girl was making a strange noise. Kind of a cross between giggling and squealing. She had a hard time catching her breath.

He slowed the rolling down, and then stopped. He lay there, staring up at the ceiling. He could feel that he had an erection.

The noises got quieter.

Lash sat up and hugged his knees. He was tired, but he felt better than he had in days.

Corporate Man was trying to catch his breath. It was clear this had pushed him to the limit. He almost couldn't keep up. But the girl had dug it. She was laughing and whooping, between breaths.

"Shit," she said. "I ain't never felt nothing like that before!"

Corporate Man's breathing slowly relaxed. He almost sounded like he was having an asthma attack there, for a few minutes. Lash worried about the man's heart.

Lash got up and got dressed. He kept his back to them.

"Did you do that?" Peroxide Girl asked. She was stretched out on the bed, and her mask had gotten lost in the action. Lash tried not to stare. She looked like a college girl, maybe nineteen. Maybe early twenties. "Hey, were you responsible for that?"

Lash went to the door and opened it.

"Shit, that was crazy," Peroxide Girl said. "I want to do this again sometime."

Lash went out and closed the door behind him. He could hear the lock click.

He wiped the sweat from his forehead with a handkerchief, and then walked down the walkway to the other end of the motel.

He had made this appointment at the last minute, and even though he had canceled the one with Cindy and told her he needed some downtime, it turned out to be a pretty good distraction.

What to do next? Lash looked across the street from the motel. There was a bar.

CHAPTER TWENTY-NINE

"Hi," Lash said. "I wasn't expecting to hear from you so soon."

"I hope it's okay," Joselyn said.

"You know, it's funny. I don't remember giving you my number the last time I saw you."

"I know," she said, and hesitated a bit. "I got your number from Antony's little black book. I wasn't going to use it; I was going to wait for you to call me. But I just got impatient, I guess. I'm really sorry about that."

"It's okay," he said. "I was just curious."

"I didn't want to be pushy," she said. "But it was a rough weekend."

"How did the funeral go?"

"Like I said, it was rough. Can we change the subject?"

"Sure."

"Are you free this afternoon?"

"You know, I just came back from a client, and I'm pretty exhausted," he took a pull from the beer bottle and made her wait a few seconds. "Can we do this tomorrow?"

"Tomorrow's fine," Joselyn said. "Really. That's great."

"Good," he pulled her card out of his wallet. "This address on your card, is that where you want me to go?"

"Sure," she said. "That's great you still have my card. I was afraid you'd lost it."

"Nope, I've got it right here." He read the address to her, just to be sure.

"That's it," she said. "What time can you get here tomorrow?"

"Let's say around noon. Is that okay? I tend to sleep late."

"Noon is fine," she said. "More than fine."

He quoted her an amount, and she accepted. He made sure it was a little higher than what Antony used to pay him. She had no trouble with it.

"Good, so I'll see you tomorrow at noon."

He was going to ask her how many people would be there, but it didn't really matter. One or twenty, it was all the same to him.

"I can't wait," she said. "Thanks a lot for not being mad at me, Lash."

"How could I ever be mad at you?" he said, smiling into the phone as he said it. *Turning on the charm.*

They exchanged good-byes and he hung up.

He erased Joselyn's message from the answering machine and found himself wondering if Miranda ever listened to his messages.

He also wondered why someone like Joselyn had been in his neighborhood last week, in the liquor store he always went to. It didn't seem like her style. He didn't live in a bad area, but she certainly seemed out of place here. Didn't she have liquor stores in the ritzy part of town where she lived? Was it really a coincidence she ran into him that day, or was it all her plan to snag his services now that Antony was out of the picture?

It didn't really matter. He liked her and liked the idea of taking her on as a client.

And that made him think of Cindy. How they'd gone beyond the client thing. How he would be seeing her again on Thursday, and he wasn't sure how he should handle it. Was Joselyn going to complicate his life further?

He decided he wasn't going to let her. Cindy was different. He had had the hots for her for a long time now, since before he had even met Miranda, and he'd had a chance to get that out of his system. But things would go back to being professional, or he would stop going to Cindy's place. He would make that clear to her on Thursday.

He found himself dialing Miranda's work number. He called to say hello and see how her day was going. And tell her how much he missed her.

CHAPTER THIRTY

"Hello?"

"Lash?"

"Lizzie, is that you?"

There was silence.

Then, "I just wanted to say hi."

"I can't really talk right now."

"How's everything?"

"Fine," Lash said. "But I can't talk."

"Can we meet for lunch sometime?"

"I'm sorry, things are really busy these days," he said. "I don't want to make any plans I can't keep."

Another silence.

Lash was sure he had had this conversation a thousand times before.

"Well," she said, after a time. "I didn't want to bother you."

"Did you get my check?" he said. It burned his ass that he had to pay her alimony and still put up with this shit.

"Yes, I did. Thank you," she said. Thinking, *I don't want your fucking money. I want you!*

"Sure," he said. He started to feel sorry for her. "How's everything with you?"

"Fine," she said. "My job's as lousy as ever."

"That's why they call it a job," he said, not knowing what else to say.

"Well, I'd better not keep you."

"Thanks," he said. "When things calm down around here, maybe we can meet for lunch sometime."

He hadn't really wanted to say it, but he felt vulnerable when he heard the sadness in her voice, and he didn't want to sound like he was brushing her off.

"Do you mean that?" she asked, suddenly sounding cheery.

"Let's play it by ear," he said, trying to sound noncommittal.

"Thank you, Lash," she said. The desperation clung to her voice.

"Yeah," he said. "I really have to go now."

"Bye," she said.

"Bye."

Lash hung up the phone.

"Who was that?" Miranda asked, when he went back into the kitchen.

"It was just my ex-wife, Lizzie."

"What did she want?"

"The hell if I know," he said. "I guess we're trying to stay on friendly terms. She just wanted to say hello. She got my alimony check."

"How come I've haven't met her yet?" Miranda asked, pouring herself a drink.

"I don't know," he said. "Are you really sure you *want* to?"

"I dunno."

He leaned against the counter. "You know, sometimes I have a really hard time talking to her."

"Why?"

"I told you how she is. She always sounds so fucking desperate. So needy. Like I'm the only person in the world she can call. It's bad enough I pay her alimony. It's like I have to pay *emotional* alimony, too. I really wish she would find someone, get married, have some kids. Maybe, if she had a life of her own, she wouldn't feel the need to call me."

"You almost sound like you're afraid of her," Miranda said.

"Not afraid, really," Lash said. "But she does put me on edge. I guess I never really learned how to handle her."

"What about me?" Miranda asked. "Do you know how to handle me?"

She put her arms around him.

"What do you think?" he asked, and kissed her.

CHAPTER THIRTY-ONE

When he got off the elevator, he found another penthouse apartment, as fancy as the rest he had been in, if not more so. How many of these places were there? And was he slowly taking a tour through them all, as more rich, pampered people found out about his gift?

"Lash," Joselyn said, coming around the corner, a glass at the ready. She handed it to him and he took it. She was wearing a bright red evening gown, and she managed to look even more striking than he remembered her being.

"Gin on the rocks," she said. "Am I right?"

"It'll do," he said.

"I remembered that's what Antony said you liked."

There could have been an awkward silence then, but he wasn't in the mood to squirm. "Yeah, nice of you to remember."

"Oh, no problem at all," she said. "Come, sit down."

She brought him down into another sunken living room. He sat down on a black leather couch.

"You told me that you were named after some old cowboy star," she said, fixing herself a drink.

"You have a good memory," Lash said. "My father named me after Lash LaRue. You probably never heard of him. *King of the Bullwhip*, they used to call him."

"And did you want to be a cowboy where you were a child?"

"It was probably the first thing I was ever sure of," Lash said. "Of course, by the time I was ten, I forgot all about that and wanted to be an astronaut instead."

They laughed. It felt like the thing to do.

She sat next to him and took a sip of her drink. Then she looked him right in the eyes. "What does it feel like?"

"Excuse me?"

"When you roll around on the floor," Joselyn asked. "What does it *feel* like?"

"Not like much of anything," he said. "I kind of go into a trance."

"Are you aware of your rolling?" she asked. "Of the people around you?"

"No, I guess I kind of go numb until it's over," he said. "Most of the time, I'm not really aware of anything."

"So it isn't pleasurable for you, too?" she asked, sounding perplexed. "You don't *feel* it, too?"

"No. Like I told you, it's like being numb."

"That's awful," she said. "You should at least be able to share the pleasure."

"I don't mind, really," he said, feeling uncomfortable answering such intimate questions. He had only met her a few times, and he really didn't like being questioned like this, no matter how amazing she looked tonight.

"What's with all the questions, anyway?" he asked, wondering if it sounded confrontational. And not caring.

"I was just curious, that's all," she said. "You're just so fascinating. What you can *do*. How you've made a profession out of it."

"I'm not qualified for much else. And I sure don't have the temperament for a nine-to-five kind of job. I take advantage of my abilities because I can, because it keeps me from having to earn an honest living."

"And I'm very happy about that," she said. "That you're not afraid to share."

"I'm not afraid of much," he told her. He drained his glass. It wasn't Tanqueray. The mediciny aftertaste pegged it as Bombay Sapphire. "Will we be starting soon?"

"A couple of other people will be joining me," she said. "I hope you don't mind."

"It doesn't matter to me."

"So you like to get paid up front, right?"

"That's how it works," he said. "I find clients don't feel like moving around much after it's over."

"I totally understand," she said. "Can I freshen your drink?"

"Sure."

She took his glass and went back to the bar. She poured his drink, added ice, and then took an envelope from beneath the counter. She brought the drink and the envelope back to him and sat beside him on the sofa again.

"Are you going to count it?"

"I trust you," he said. "So when are these other people coming?"

"They're already here," she said. "In another room. Shall we join them?"

Lash took a long drink from his glass. "Yeah, okay."

She stood up and walked down a long hall. Lash followed. He was surprised he hadn't heard anything indicating they weren't alone. As he followed her, he couldn't help noticing how perfect Joselyn's ass looked beneath the tight, red fabric.

They reached a series of rooms; several had their doors closed. Lash was amazed at the sheer size of the place. Joselyn knocked on one door and called out, "Here we come!"

She opened the door and ushered Lash inside. The room was large and mostly cleared of furniture, except for a king-sized bed against the back wall. Despite the size of the bed, there was plenty of room for him on the floor.

On the bed, a blonde girl was naked and stretched out, tied to the bedposts. She was struggling slightly, but it was more like she was testing her bonds than really trying to get away. A large, burly guy was making sure the ropes were tight.

"Oh, Jesus," the girl said. "Fancy meeting you again!"

Lash had thought she looked familiar when he first came in, but now, hearing her voice, he remembered where he had met her. In that motel with "Mr. Gamble." She was the girl he had been with, the one who lost her mask. *Peroxide Girl.*

"I was hoping I'd see *you* again," she said in that nasal voice of hers.

Lash chuckled. "Good to see you again, too."

"Yeah, I didn't keep my mask on very long last time."

"So you know each other?" Joselyn asked.

"Yep," Peroxide Girl said. "We had a real interesting time

the last time we got together."

"It was another session," Lash said to Joselyn. "Another client."

"Mr. Gamble, he said his name was," the blonde said and laughed. "He was a strange one, always wearing that mask of his."

Lash didn't know if they should be discussing Mr. Gamble here. He didn't feel comfortable talking about clients to other clients.

"Who's this Mr. Gamble?" Joselyn asked. "Did Antony know him?"

"I doubt it," Lash said. "Let's just say he's a man who likes his anonymity."

"*I'll* say," Peroxide Girl said and grinned.

Joselyn didn't bother introducing anybody. Because Lash had seen her before, he assumed the blonde was from an escort service or something similar. The burly guy was very quiet and mostly seemed wrapped up in checking everything. He did not introduce himself and Joselyn didn't bother to, either.

"You want me to get ready?" Lash asked Joselyn.

"Sure, we're just about ready ourselves."

Lash went over to the open space and started to undress. He could see on the side where the man was now. The guy was only wearing a robe, that was half-open. On the carpet near him were various sex toys. Dildoes and vibrators of various sizes. And other things. Weird devices Lash had never seen before, which was odd, because he thought he had seen everything at this point. And some tools. Pliers. Clamps. And a red metal toolbox that probably held more surprises.

A kinky bunch, Lash thought as he unbuttoned his shirt.

He folded his clothes and put them over near the window. He was standing there in his underwear and he went to find a comfortable spot on the plush carpeting. As he sat down, he glanced over at the bed. The guy had already started going down on Peroxide Girl, and she was squirming. The guy's robe was off and his body was muscular. Joselyn was nude now as well and was working on the girl's breasts with her mouth.

Lash removed his boxers and got down on the carpet. He

slowly rocked back and forth, letting the trance come and take him over.

As the trance slowly enveloped him, taking him over, he could hear Peroxide Girl's moans getting louder.

He closed his eyes and everything went numb and silent as he let the rocking and rolling take him over.

At one point, he almost came out of it. He could have sworn he heard a scream. But it had to be a sound of pleasure and he tried to get back to the trance.

There was another scream, and then he lost consciousness again.

"Do you think he heard anything?"

"No. When he goes into that trance of his, I don't think he hears anything at all."

One of the voices was definitely male. The other one was Joselyn.

Lash was curled in a ball on the carpet. He kept his eyes closed.

"What a mess," the man said. "How the fuck are we going to clean this up?"

"Just get her out of here," Joselyn said. "I'll take care of it."

Lash listened to the sounds. He noticed he was shaking. And he wondered how long he had been unconscious. He felt more disoriented than usual. He heard what sounded like the man leaving the room. His heavy footsteps were muffled by the carpet.

Then Joselyn must have been moving around the bed. Gathering things. Removing sheets.

Lash lay there, wondering when it would be okay to open his eyes and move.

He decided to wait a bit longer.

"You were knocked out a long time," Joselyn said when he came into the living room.

After all the activity had finally died down and they'd left him alone, he waited another half hour before getting up and putting on his clothes. He noticed the bed had been stripped of sheets, but otherwise there wasn't anything too suspicious. Except for a small stain on one edge of the mattress, which looked like blood.

"Yeah," he said. "For some reason the trance lasted awhile this time."

"We had a great time," Joselyn said. "It was money well spent."

"I'm glad," he said, not knowing what else to say. He still had the envelope in his pants pocket. There was no reason to stay any longer.

She motioned to a full glass on the glass coffee table. "I took the liberty of making you another drink."

He wanted to leave, but he figured a drink would calm him a bit. And for some reason he felt the need to get a sense of where Joselyn's head was at right now. If she gave away any hints that something weird had just happened.

Lash went over to where she sat and sat nearby. He lifted the drink.

It smelled strongly of gin. He almost wondered if there might be something else in it. *Something to keep him quiet.* Would they dispose of him as easily as they did the blonde girl?

He noticed his hand was shaking slightly and didn't want her to see that. So he brought the glass quickly to his lips.

"You really did need a drink, didn't you?"

"It was an especially strong trance this time," Lash said. "I feel like I was out cold for hours."

"Three hours, to be exact," Joselyn said. "I was actually starting to get a bit worried."

Was she worried? Or did he hear relief in her voice that he hadn't woken earlier to interrupt her *cleaning*?

"Three? Man, that's weird," Lash said.

"Yeah, the others left about an hour ago. They seemed pretty happy, though."

"Good," he finished his drink, and started to get up.

"You sure you don't want another one?"

"I've really got to go," Lash said. "I have somebody waiting for me. I'm late as it is."

"I was hoping maybe we could talk about doing this again.

If you're happy with the money arrangement, I mean."

"I still feel kind of tired," Lash said, getting to his feet. "Give me a call sometime and we'll talk about it more then. Okay?"

"Okay," she said, sounding disappointed. "If that's what you'd prefer." She frowned slightly.

"I'd appreciate it," he said. "I still feel a bit out of sorts."

"Let me walk you to the elevator," Joselyn said.

She led him down the hall again and pushed the "down" button on the wall.

"I hope you can come back soon," she said. "I think what you do is amazing."

"Yeah," Lash said. "Thanks."

They both stood there for what seemed like forever, until there was a soft bell sound, and the elevator door opened.

She leaned forward then and put her arms around his neck. She kissed him. He could feel her tongue trying to find its way into his mouth and he resisted at first, then he decided it was better to play along.

When she was done, she pulled away. "I really had a great time," she said.

He forced a smile and got inside the elevator. He pushed the button for the lobby.

She waved to him as the door closed. He stood there, with a fake smile frozen on his lips.

He breathed a great sigh of relief when the door closed completely and he started moving down.

CHAPTER THIRTY-TWO

Lash did feel a little disoriented in the cab home, and when he got back to his apartment, he saw he was still shaking. He poured himself a fresh drink and sat down in front of the television.

He stared at the blank screen as he drank.

What the hell happened in there? he wondered. *Did anything bad happen to that girl or was she just particularly vocal? Should I worry about this at all?*

One thing he didn't want to do was go back to Joselyn's place. But if he refused to go there again, would it look suspicious? Like he thought he had witnessed something?

It didn't matter. *I'm not going back*, he thought.

He drained the glass and poured himself another one.

It was then that he heard the screaming.

It seemed to come from everywhere, and he almost dropped the glass. Somehow, he was able to put it down on the counter before he lost complete control of his hand.

The screaming got louder, and he found himself huddled on the floor, hugging his knees tightly, trying to ride it out.

The screaming was replaced with voices. Whispering, almost inhuman voices, that said things he couldn't understand.

And then the screams again.

Somehow, he had gotten up and gone into the kitchen, although he didn't remember it. He found himself rolling around on the floor, banging against the cupboard and the table.

And then he went into another trance.

He came out of it before Miranda got home. He got up off the floor and went to the bathroom. He turned the shower on and got undressed. Lash got under the warm spray and tried to blank his mind.

He remembered Joselyn's kiss. He could feel it still.

He rubbed soap on his skin, and saw his hand was *still* shaking.

Lash closed his eyes tightly as he washed himself. He was afraid if he opened them, the howling, terror-stricken face of Peroxide Girl would pop out at him from the tile walls of the shower stall.

Something bad must have happened back in that place. The last time he had felt so weird was after he had found Antony swinging by a rope. There had to have been more death around him.

This made him think back to the gas station bathroom, back on that weekend when he and Miranda had gone away. When he went in there, he almost went into a trance against his will. It had taken all his effort to snap out of it. Someone must have died in there sometime before he went inside. Maybe the night before.

Death.

It had some kind of weird reaction on his *ability*.

He felt waves of cold shivers run through his body, and he turned the water hotter, trying to chase them away.

CHAPTER THIRTY-THREE

"A re you okay?" Miranda asked. "You look really pale."

He could still feel the vomit taste in the back of his throat. After his shower, he had gotten sick for a while. It kept threatening to happen again. He looked down at his plate and concentrated on keeping his stomach stable.

"You really do look sick," Miranda said. "I'm worried about you."

"I just need some sleep," he said. "Must be something going around."

"This is like that time after Antony died," she said.

"It's just the flu or something. I'll be fine."

"Did something unusual happen today?"

"Not really," he said. "I just saw a client, that's all."

"Lash, we've really got to talk," she said, looking very serious.

"What about?"

"I want to know what you *do* with these clients of yours. It just makes me worry more, not knowing. I have an inkling. You said some things the night Antony died."

"What did I say?"

"I wish you'd be honest with me," Miranda said. "I can take it."

"It's really hard to explain," he said. "I've been putting it off, because I really don't know how to explain it."

"Try," she said.

He couldn't bear the thought of eating. He picked up his beer bottle instead and took a long pull.

"Years ago, I found out I had this weird *ability*," he told her. "It was very strange. I stumbled upon it by accident."

"What kind of ability?"

"I kind of roll around on the floor, and I go into a kind of trance," he said, trying to find the words. Words that made sense. "And this trance, it *affects* other people."

"How?" she said. He could see the frustration in her face, like getting the answer out of him was like pulling teeth. But part of him didn't want to tell her, and another part of him didn't know how to make sense of it.

He thought of Lizzie. How she had become addicted to what he could do, and how that changed their relationship. Ruined it. It would be easier just to show Miranda what he did, but he didn't want to go there. Not *now*. He felt strange, like something was happening inside him, and he wanted to just crawl into a ball somewhere.

What happened back at Joselyn's place, anyway? He wondered. *Did that girl really* die *today?*

"Lash?" Miranda said. "Please don't zone out like that. You were going to tell me how your trance affects other people."

"It heightens sensations," he said, taking another pull of his beer. "*Sexual* sensations mostly."

"I don't understand."

"I roll around on the floor and these clients of mine, they have sex. And what I do makes their sensations stronger. It amplifies everything."

She stared at him. "You're kidding me. I have never heard anything like that before."

"I've never been more serious in my life."

"So you have sex with these people?" she wanted to know.

"No," he said. "It doesn't work that way. When I'm in the trance, I'm useless. I'm numb. I'm outside myself. So I don't really interact with them at all. I'm usually off to one side, away from them but in the same room."

"That is the strangest thing I ever heard of."

"That's why I didn't tell you for so long. I didn't know how to tell you and it make *sense*. Most people who know about it, they've *felt* it, but it's a hard thing to put into words."

"Look, it's been really good when we make love," she told him. "I can't deny that. You've made me feel things I never felt before. I just figured you knew some tricks. But I can't believe that you go into a trance and stimulate people that way..."

"You've felt a bit of it when we do it," he said. "But you've never felt the full effect."

"And you do this with people, for money?"

"Yeah," he said. "It actually pays very well."

"Can I?" she asked him.

He hesitated. "Can you what?"

"Can you make me feel the *full effect*, as you call it? I just want to see for myself. It's so hard to believe this."

He thought of Lizzie and how it had ruined at least one relationship, but at the same time, he wanted to share his ability with her. He wanted to make her *feel* it. Like he said, there were no words to really describe it. In order to understand, she had to experience it.

"Okay," he said. "Just do what I tell you."

"Where are you going?"

"Just get undressed and listen to me," he said.

He pushed the coffee table out of the way and crawled onto the living room carpet. Luckily, the apartment had a plush, soft weave of carpeting, but even then he got burns sometimes. Miranda stretched out on the sofa.

"Start touching yourself," he said.

"Are you serious?"

"Miranda, you wanted to experience it. You have to do what I tell you. In order for this to work, you have to participate. You can't just lie there."

He listened for the sounds that told him she was doing it, and slowly he began to roll back and forth. Eventually, his eyes closed and he entered the trance state. He had no idea how long he was rolling before his eyes opened and he vomited on the floor.

It took her a few minutes to realize something was wrong, and she had to recover from the sensations he was making her feel before she could move. She leaned over the side of the sofa.

"You're still sick," she said.

"Yeah, I guess I'm still not myself yet. I need more sleep."

"Let me clean you up."

"Did you feel it?" he asked her.

"Yes," she said. "It was…" Her words trailed off.

"I told you," he said. "Just wait until I feel better. It will blow the top of your head off."

"If you don't feel better soon, maybe you should make an appointment with your doctor," she said.

There's nothing a doctor could do, he thought. *He wouldn't have a clue where to start.*

Lash excused himself and then went down the hallway to the bedroom. He got undressed, shut off the light, and crawled into bed.

Not long afterward, Miranda crawled in beside him and hugged him close.

CHAPTER THIRTY-FOUR

L ash kept his appointment with Cindy.

He had slept late into the morning. Somehow, when he woke up, he didn't feel as bad. But he really needed to get out of the apartment and see someone he felt comfortable with. Someone who didn't question him.

And he had to admit that Cindy fit the bill right now.

She met him at the elevator and took his coat. The apartment hadn't changed. It was still elegant. He felt uncomfortable moving around in it, afraid he might accidentally knock something over.

Cindy was wearing a sheer nightgown, and nothing under it. The way she acted made him think she was high on something. But she knew he wasn't into drugs, so she didn't offer him any. He had turned them down before, the times she had been with Antony.

"Can I get you anything?" she asked. "Gin?"

"Sure," he said, wondering how many gallons of gin he had consumed in his lifetime. *Oceans* of gin. And everyone seemed to have it handy. It was kind of like a joke and he almost started laughing.

"Thanks for coming," she said as she went over to the bar.

"Well, we did have an appointment," he said.

"I know, but I know things have been a little crazy for you," she said. "And you did find Antony after all."

The name sent a shiver through him. He didn't really feel like talking about Antony right now, but he couldn't think of anything else to talk about.

"Did you go to the funeral?" he asked.

"Yes, I did," she said. "It was really small. There were only a few close friends there."

"I'm sorry I couldn't make it," Lash said.

"You really don't have to explain," she said. "I really do understand. I almost didn't go myself."

He thought of the conversation he had had with Joselyn. But he didn't want to bring her up. *Not here.*

"Shouldn't we steer this conversation in a different direction?" Lash asked. "I mean, funerals aren't the kind of topic to get things in the mood."

"I guess not," she said, grabbing his hand and leading him down the hall. "Lash, are you living with someone?"

"Yeah," Lash said. "Why?"

"I called you once and a woman answered," Cindy said. "I didn't want to cause any problems, so I hung up. I didn't say a word."

"You're a client," he said. "Don't worry about calling me."

"You sounded uncomfortable the last time we spoke on the phone. I got a vibe, I guess, not to cause any problems," she said.

"I just had a lot on my mind then," Lash said.

"You said I'm a client," Cindy said. "Is that all I am?"

He looked down at her hand, holding his.

"I don't know."

"What kind of answer is that?"

"Listen, I don't really know what I feel right now," Lash said. "But I didn't come here to talk about it, okay? You asked me here for a reason, didn't you?"

"I wanted to see you," Cindy said. "That's the main reason why I asked you here. And I don't want to be thought of as just another client."

She put his hand between her legs. He did not resist.

"I want you to take off your clothes," she told him.

"Is someone else here?" Lash asked. "Or are you alone again?"

"I'm not alone," she told him. "You're here."

She led him by the hand to a room at the end of the hall. They went inside. There was no furniture, not even a bed. The carpet was thick and looked like polar bear fur, but it wasn't. It was soft and plush. In the middle of the room, there was a pile of colorful objects.

"What did you have in mind for this time?" he asked.

She walked over to the pile. She picked up a few items and walked back to him.

"Put this on your head."

It was a kind of headgear. It was soft, foam rubber. He put it on. It did not hinder his breathing.

She put on a similar helmet.

Cindy walked back to the middle of the room. She got down on the carpet. The rest of the pile was made up of rubber pads for other parts of the body. She spread them out on the carpet.

He got undressed. She removed her nightgown.

"Come here," she said.

He walked over and knelt beside her on the floor.

"Put these on," she told him.

"What is all this?" he asked.

"They're pads I picked up," she said. "They're used for various kinds of fighting."

"Are we going to fight?"

"No," she said. "We're going to fuck."

They strapped pads onto each other. Arm pads. Kneepads. Shin pads. Back pads.

It was like an elaborate ritual.

"I still don't get it," he told her.

"I want to roll with you," she said. "With you *inside* me."

"I tried something like this once," he told her. "It wasn't as involved as all this, but..."

He hesitated.

"It didn't work all that well."

"So, you can't try more than once?" she asked. "Maybe it wasn't the right person last time. Even if it doesn't work, we can still have normal sex, can't we?"

"It doesn't bother you that I'm living with someone?" he asked.

She looked into his eyes.

"Does it bother you?"

He didn't answer. He had lied about trying it before. Sure, he had done a little rocking while he was in the sack, but he never let himself go into a trance, and he never tried anything like this. She had really thought this through, and it sounded like it might actually work. And that scared him.

Despite the helmets, their mouths were exposed. She kissed him.

He could feel her hand on his erect cock. She put the head inside her and slid down on the shaft.

"Hold me close," she said.

He held her. He was on his back. She was on top. There was a Velcro strap around their waists, holding them together. She fastened it and embraced him tightly.

"Roll," she said.

He began to roll. *They* began to roll.

"Faster," she said.

He rolled faster.

The helmets prevented them from banging their heads together. The other pads protected their bodies.

They rolled over. He was on top now.

He felt himself on the edge of a trance, looking into her face. He tried to resist. He wanted to feel her. To watch her face.

She was breathing hard, grunting. And so was he.

He gave in to the trance.

CHAPTER THIRTY-FIVE

L ash came out of it.
   He was still wearing his helmet. So was she. The Velcro strap was still holding the two of them together.

Her eyes were closed. At first, he was afraid he had killed her somehow.

He stared at her eyelids. Eventually, she opened them.

She kissed him, then went limp again.

They just lay there on the carpet, for what seemed like hours.

Then she unstrapped them. He let her move away. She collapsed beside him.

"Did it work?" he whispered.

"My God," she said, stretching out on her side.

They were both soaked with sweat.

"Don't you remember any of it?" she asked.

"No," he said.

"No?" she asked. "You don't know what you missed, baby! That was the best one yet."

She had her back to him, and she didn't move.

He touched her.

"What was it like?"

"Like an atom bomb, baby!" she said, softly. "Like fucking Armageddon."

She started to sit up.

"Shit," she said. "It looks like you came a hundred times."

There was big puddle of his come, dripping out of her. Semen was thick in his pubic hair. But he hadn't felt any of it.

"Let's take a shower," she said.

She tried to stand up, and almost fell. He had to support her, lift her to her feet.

She held onto him, led him down the hall to the bathroom. It was huge. The shower was encased in a big glass booth, easily big enough for two people, maybe more. She stumbled over to the shower and turned it on.

He stood, in dazed silence, listening to the shower, feeling the steam that swirled out from behind the glass.

She took his hand and led him inside.

CHAPTER THIRTY-SIX

"You're late," Miranda said, when he got back.

"I was at a job," he said. "Sometimes it runs late."

"I had no idea when you'd be back," she explained. "Are you hungry?"

"Yeah," he said. "But don't go to any trouble. I can fix something for myself."

He took his coat off and tossed it on the sofa as he passed it on the way to the kitchen. He opened the refrigerator and saw a casserole dish containing ravioli from the night before. He took it out and popped it into the microwave. He punched the buttons.

"I was worried," he was told.

"I'm sorry," he said. "Things like this don't happen too often, but they happen. I can't really give you a call and let you know when I'll be late."

"I guess I don't understand *why* you can't call. I wanted to go out tonight, to a movie," she said. "But now it's too late."

"Didn't I already explain all this?" he asked. "I go into a trance. I lose track of time. It's not an exact science where I can set an alarm. It's outside my control, and so sometimes I get home late."

She pouted. He would have found it cute if he wasn't so annoyed with her.

"I said I was sorry."

Lash stood in front of the microwave, watching it work, waiting for it to finish zapping his food. "It's just as well. I'm tired as hell."

The microwave beeped. He took the casserole dish out. It was hot and burned his fingers. He almost dropped it. He got the lid off and got a fork from the drawer.

The food was too hot to eat. He had to let it cool anyway.

"Lash, what would do you if I asked you to stop doing this?" she asked him. "If I asked you to get a real job."

"Don't ask me that," he said. He grew impatient with the hot food and put the dish in the sink to cool. "You might not like the answer."

"Why can't you have a normal job, like anyone else?"

"Because I had a normal job, I had a few of them, and it was like serving my time in hell. I have a talent, so I use it. That's all. And it pays great. Why should I go back to a lifestyle I can't stand, that used to keep me depressed all the time, just because you have a hang-up about what I do for a living?"

"Do you ever sleep with your clients?" she asked.

"This again. I told you," he said. "There's no contact. They don't touch me; I don't touch them. That's the way it works. I'm not a male whore, for Christ's sake."

"What happens?" she asked. "Tell me again. Tell me in detail."

"What is this, the fucking Inquisition?"

"Tell me about tonight."

"I'm so fucking tired," he said. He took the dish out of the sink and brought into the other room and sat down in front of the television and ate ravioli. It was still hot and burned the inside of his mouth, but he didn't pay attention to that.

"You just roll around on the floor while other people fuck, is that it?"

"I told you already. Look, I don't like to discuss my work. I don't feel right talking about it. And besides, it seems to upset you."

"I wish you'd never told me."

The feeling's mutual, he thought. But he didn't say it. He remembered her words the night before. "I wish you'd be honest with me. *I can take it.*"

The food burned his tongue, but he gulped it down fast.

"Why won't you talk about it?" she said.

"You just said you wish I hadn't told you."

"But you did," she said. "And I want to know it all, now."

"What do you want me to say?"

She was standing in front of the television, blocking his view. She turned around and shut it off.

"Tell me about tonight. Tell me it *all*."

"I go someplace. Usually there's two people. Sometimes it's an orgy. I get down on the floor and I go into a trance. It's kind of like a fit or something. I'm completely out of it. What they're doing while I'm out of it, I couldn't care less."

"I was looking through your appointment book," Miranda said. "You marked down somebody's name for today. Someone named Cindy."

"Yeah, so? If it was a secret, then I'd hide it, right?" he said, and thought, *Why the fuck* didn't *I hide that thing?*

"You have female clients and you want me to believe you didn't fuck her?"

"Just about every time I do this, there are women there," he said. "Once in a while, it's just men, but not too often. And the women aren't crawling all over me. They're occupied, see? I'm just a piece of furniture. They don't even notice me. They just notice what I *do* for them."

"So you've never fucked a client?"

"Look, maybe when I wasn't involved with anyone, maybe I got in on some of it. But that's not the case now, is it? Are you accusing me of something or what?"

"What a fucked-up way to earn a living," she said.

"What brought all this on?" he asked. "I'm late one time since you moved in here, and you start accusing me of shit. What is this stupidity?"

"Now I'm stupid," Miranda said, glaring at him.

"Just get the fuck off my back," he said. "I earn good money what I'm doing. It pays the bills. It's better than any fucking normal job. And that's that. You got a problem with it, that's just too bad!"

She ran to the bedroom and slammed the door as loudly as she could.

CHAPTER THIRTY-SEVEN

L ash woke up to find himself in bed alone.
He sat up and walked over to the bedroom door. When he had climbed into bed, it was late and Miranda had been asleep.

He opened the door and walked down the hall.

He could hear Miranda retching.

Lash tried to be as quiet as possible. He stood outside the bathroom door, listening to her vomit.

After a few minutes, he gently opened the door.

Lash stood there, in the doorway, watching her. She did not seem aware of him as she held her head over the toilet bowl.

Lash approached her. She was only wearing her pajama tops. He slid off his shorts.

He put his hands on her shoulders. She was tense. She did not turn to face him.

Instead, she vomited again. The room smelled of it.

He waited until she had stopped retching for a moment, and then he moved her body, so that he could enter her from behind. He did it slowly, ready to move if she tried to push him away. She didn't.

His hands were on her shoulders. She seemed to relax, but still she did not turn to look at him. Her breathing was uneven. Trying to hold back the heaves.

Then suddenly, she began to struggle. She tried to push him away, but he held on to her. He had promised himself that he would stop if she resisted, but now that it was happening, he found that he couldn't bring himself to disengage from her.

Eventually, she stopped fighting and gave into him. She let him enter her again. They both moved away from the toilet bowl. They were fucking on the linoleum floor.

He held her sides and increased the momentum.

He came and pulled out of her. His semen spilled onto the tile. But it wasn't much. He had expended most of it in Cindy.

Her head went down into her hands. She was sobbing.

"Miranda," he said softly. "Are you okay?"

"That was disgusting," she said softly. "Go back to bed."

"Miranda?"

"Please," she said. This time she sounded more assertive.

"Okay," he said. He stood up and grabbed some toilet paper. He wiped his penis and threw the rolled-up paper in the toilet. He grabbed another piece and was going to wipe the floor.

"Just get out, okay?" she said, sounding impatient. "I'll clean up in here."

"Are you sure?"

"Please," she said again. This time she turned around to face him. There were tears on her cheeks.

He dropped the paper and left the bathroom.

He went into the bedroom and closed the door. He got into bed, waiting for her to come back.

She didn't.

After a while, he drifted back to sleep.

CHAPTER THIRTY-EIGHT

When Lash woke again, he was still alone.

He looked at the clock. It was close to nine in the morning. He got up and went out into the hall. The bathroom door was open. Miranda wasn't in there.

He walked throughout the apartment. There was no sign of her.

There was a folded letter on top of the television.

He read it softly to himself.

"I had to leave," he read. "I don't think living together is working out. I need some time alone to think."

He called her cell phone. It rang and rang with no answer. No answering message came on either. He hung up.

Lash went back to the bedroom and looked in the closet. Her things were gone. Things of hers that had been in the drawers were also missing. He wondered when she had had time to pack them all. Had she packed before he even came to bed the night before and stashed her suitcase in the closet for later? Had she packed while he was sleeping? In the long run, it didn't really matter.

And *why* had she left? Had it been the scene last night in the bathroom? Had it been because of what he did for a living? Did she somehow find out about what happened at Cindy's place?

No, there was no way she could know *that*.

The guilt was getting to him, making him paranoid.

He had no idea what was on Miranda's mind. But he was determined to find her and talk things out.

He was getting dressed when the phone rang.

He ran to answer it.

"Miranda?" he asked.

"No, Lash, it's Cindy."

"Oh, hi," he said.

"You sound disappointed," she said. "Is everything okay?"

"Sorry about that. Things are just a little crazy on this end," he told her. "What's up?"

"We have to talk about things…"

"I can't really do this right now," he interrupted.

"Then it will have to wait until I get back," she finished. "We can talk then. I have to leave town for a little while. But I really think we have to talk."

"How long will you be gone?" Lash asked.

"About a week or so," she said. "It's a family emergency."

"Nothing too awful, I hope."

"Someone's died," Cindy said, but wouldn't elaborate. "I have to go to the West Coast."

"I'm sorry to hear it."

"I just wanted to let you know," she said. "I'll call you when I get back and we can arrange to meet. Okay?"

"Okay," he said. "Just call my cell and let me know." Then, "Cindy, did you try to call me yesterday? After I left, did you call here at all?"

"No," she said. "I didn't. Why, is something wrong?"

"No," he said. "I was just wondering."

"Well, I have to go now," Cindy said. "My flight leaves soon and I have to get ready."

"Sure," he said.

They exchanged good-byes and hung up.

Out of pure frustration, Lash tried to call Miranda again. Maybe he had called the wrong number before. But he hadn't. There still wasn't any answer. It just kept ringing and ringing.

He finished dressing and then left.

CHAPTER THIRTY-NINE

L ash stood in front of the door to Miranda's old apartment. He knocked.

No answer.

He knocked again, louder this time, but still there was no response.

He had the key she had given him a while back, before they moved into his place together. He turned the key in the lock.

The apartment was dark and looked the same way they had left it when he had helped her move some of her stuff to his place. All her furniture was still there. He searched the rooms, but there was sign of her. As far as he could tell, she had not been back here for a long time.

He left the apartment, locking the door on his way out.

Lash stood in the hallway, not knowing where else to go.

He decided to take a cab back to his apartment and wait for Miranda to call.

CHAPTER FORTY

There were no messages on his machine when he got back. Lash had a little book of phone numbers, and some of Miranda's friends were listed in it. He looked them up and called.

None of them knew where Miranda was. Or, if they did, they weren't telling him.

After the last call, Lash realized that he had no alternative but to wait. Maybe she would change her mind and come back. At least give him a chance to explain.

He got a bottle of beer from the refrigerator and turned on the television. He sat down to watch, and noticed Miranda's letter, still on top of the set.

He did not read it a second time.

Staring at the folded letter from where he sat, he was overcome with incredible anger. He shook violently in his chair.

He looked down at his hands. They were clenched fists.

The next thing he knew, he was down on the floor, rolling. As he rolled, he struck furniture, banging his body and his head, but he did not feel it. He was on the edge of a trance.

He could see Antony up above him, hanging from the ceiling. Dead.

"Dead dead dead dead dead," Lash repeated over and over as he rolled across the living room floor, oblivious to his surroundings and the things he collided with.

The anger subsided and was replaced with an overwhelming sense of fear.

The fear engulfed him, and then the trance took over completely.

He lost focus and fell into the void.

CHAPTER FORTY-ONE

"Dead dead dead dead dead," Lash was chanting, as he opened his eyes and saw.

His head was in someone's lap. A hand was stroking his cheek.

"Miranda?" he asked.

The person did not answer. He tilted his head back to look up at a face.

Lizzie's.

"You," he said, sitting up suddenly. "What are you doing here?"

"I was worried," she said. "I knocked on your door, but you wouldn't answer. And I could hear you thrashing around in here."

"How did you know I wasn't fucking someone?" Lash asked, feeling the anger again. "And how did you get in here? The door was locked."

"I had a spare key," she said. "I didn't remember getting another copy made, but I guess I did. I happened to have it in my purse, and, like I said, I was concerned. It didn't sound like any fucking I'd ever heard."

"Just get out," Lash said, getting to his feet. He held on to the side of the sofa for support at first. It took a minute to maintain his sense of balance.

"Is this how you treat someone who was trying to help you?" Lizzie asked.

"No one asked you to come here," he said. "I just want to be left alone!"

"I've been here for a while now," she told him. "At first, I couldn't calm you down at all, you were just rolling around like a madman. Then, finally, you stopped. I've been trying to revive you ever since. I was almost going to call an ambulance. You were in an awful state. But I knew what you were doing, and I wanted to give you time to come out of it on your own."

"Well, I'm out of it now," he said. "You know how my trances are. I can't predict how long they'll last. But I don't need an ambulance and I don't need you."

"Where's Miranda?"

"That's none of your business," he said.

"Such hostility! I'm only trying to help."

"I don't want your help. I told you, I want to be left alone. I'll be fine."

"I wish I could believe you," Lizzie said. "But this whole thing has me spooked. I'd never seen you in a trance like that before. It was worse than anything I'd ever seen.

More violent. You looked like you were having a seizure. Or were a man possessed."

"It's none of your concern," he said. "I told you to get out, didn't I?"

"Why won't you let me help you?" Lizzie asked, standing up as well. She looked injured. "Miranda isn't here to help you, so why can't I?"

"Stop mentioning Miranda," Lash said. "I told you, it's none of your business where she is."

"She's gone," Lizzie said. "That's what brought this episode on. That's why you're treating me like this."

"No, she's not gone," Lash said. "She'll be back. I just don't like you breaking into my apartment. We talked about this before, don't you remember?"

"Miranda's gone," Lizzie said. "I know she is. I looked around when I found you. I saw that note she left you."

"Shut up!" he said. "This is none of your business!"

"No, I won't shut up," Lizzie said. "And I won't leave. Not until I know for sure that you're all right."

"I told you to get the fuck out of here, didn't I?" he shouted.

He approached her and grabbed her arm.

Lizzie screamed. It was short but loud.

Lash pulled away, letting go of her.

"Shut up!" he shouted. "Stop that fucking screaming! Just get out. That's all I want. I don't want you here. All this time, I've been trying to keep it inside me. I didn't want to hurt you any more than I had to. But now you've provoked me. I don't want anything to do with you anymore. I have no place for you in my life."

"You're upset," Lizzie said. "You don't know what you're saying."

"Yes, I do."

"You said you didn't want to hurt me," Lizzie said. "But don't you realize how much you hurt me when you wanted to divorce? When you rejected me? You can't hurt me any more than that."

"I can punch you in the fucking face if you don't get out of here," he said. But his voice was less angry now.

"Despite what little you think of me," Lizzie said. "I'm here. I care. Where's your Miranda?"

"Stop trying to insert yourself back in my life," Lash said. "This has nothing to do with you. I'm done with you."

"When you calm down, you'll realize how loyal I am," she said. "How I stand by you. How I'm always here for you."

"You must be deaf," Lash said, shaking his head. "Deaf and stupid."

"You're just shaken up," Lizzie said. "You were surprised to wake up and see me here when you thought you were alone. And you were scared by what had happened to you. I don't blame you."

"I need time to think about things," Lash said. "Time alone. I don't want you here."

"But I don't want to leave you," she said. "You may need me. What if it happens again? Miranda isn't here to take care of you."

"For Christ's sake, I'm a grown man!" Lash said. "I can take care of myself. I can deal with my problems by myself. I don't need someone to take care of me. Not Miranda. Not you. Not anyone. Just because you're so fucking needy doesn't mean that everyone else is. Doesn't mean that I am."

"We all need help now and then," she said. "Even you."

Lash walked over toward the wall. He had his back to her. "If I went into another trance, there's nothing you could do anyway. Nothing either one of us could do, except wait it out. That blows your theory about being able to help me. So just get out."

"No."

He rammed one of his fists into the wall. A framed picture fell off the wall, onto the floor. The glass shattered.

"Get out, god dammit!"

"No."

He drummed on the wall with his fists. His eyes were closed. His teeth were clenched.

When he was done, he opened his eyes. His hands were bleeding. He turned. Lizzie was still standing in the same spot, staring at him.

"You're bleeding," she said.

"No shit," he said. "I'm bleeding."

She moved towards him. "Let me help you."

"Get the fuck away from me!" Lash said. "Haven't you been listening to a word I said? I don't want you here. I don't want you here!"

Lizzie moved forward and grasped one of his wrists.

"Let me help you."

He wanted to scream, to lash out at her.

But he felt a violent shiver run through him, and there were spots in front of his eyes. Aftereffects from the trance, no doubt. He felt dazed and almost lost his balance.

She led him to the bathroom and washed his wounds.

CHAPTER FORTY-TWO

"Do you want me to find out where she is?" Lizzie asked. Lash was in bed. She was sitting on the bed beside him.

He felt weak. Helpless.

"Do you want me to find Miranda for you?" Lizzie asked. "I will, if you want me to."

Lash stared up at the ceiling.

"I'd even do that," she said. "To prove to you how much I care."

"You can't find her," he said, finally.

"Yes, I can," she said. Confident. Positive.

"Do what the fuck you want. Just get away from me."

"I'll find her."

His knuckles were wrapped in bandages. The room was slowly getting dark.

"I'll find her," Lizzie said again. "I promise you that."

Then, she left the room.

He sat in bed, waiting for her to leave. Waiting for the sounds of her leaving.

A few minutes later, he heard the front door close. And lock.

Lash got out of bed.

I have to get that fucking lock changed, he thought, as he walked down the hall, almost stumbling.

He went into the kitchen and found a fresh bottle of bourbon in one of the lower cabinets.

He broke the seal.

CHAPTER FORTY-THREE

Lash knew that Miranda's family lived somewhere in California. She hadn't talked about them much. In fact, she tended to avoid the subject. He had never met them or spoken to them on the phone. But he decided to try to reach them, thinking that maybe they might have the answer to where Miranda had gone.

He had no idea what her parents' names were, but he remembered that her brother's name was Paul. He lived in or near Los Angeles. She had mentioned him once, in passing.

He talked to a series of operators and asked for listings for Paul Jameson. There were dozens of them. He had asked an operator for the numbers, and he called each of them, one after another. When none of them turned out to be the right one, he called another operator. He lost track of how many people he had called. None of them were Miranda's brother.

As he called, he took swigs of bourbon.

The operators grew increasingly annoyed with him. Sick of him calling over and over again for numbers. And he was getting tired of it himself.

After a while, he gave up. It was futile. He didn't even know if her brother lived in California anymore. And he had no idea how to reach her parents.

He sat there, by the phone, waiting. For what, he wasn't sure.

Eventually, he fell asleep.

It was the next morning when he woke to the sound of his phone ringing.

He picked it up.

It was Lizzie.

"I found out where she is," Lizzie said.

"What?" he asked, not sure if he heard her right. "Where is she?"

"She's in the hospital."

"The hospital?" Lash asked. "What the hell for?"

"Complications brought on by bulimia," Lizzie said. "Cedar Hills Hospital."

Lash took a swig from the bottle.

"How do you know this?"

Lizzie didn't answer.

"Do you know what room she's in?" Lash asked.

"No, that's all I know."

"Thanks," Lash said.

"I promised you I'd find her," Lizzie said.

Before she could say anything else, he hung up on her.

He dialed the hospital.

The woman he spoke to was reluctant to give him any information, but he was able to figure out that Miranda was there.

"She isn't seeing visitors at this time," the woman told him. "And when she does, it will be immediate family only."

Lash hung up the phone.

"We'll see about that," he said to himself.

CHAPTER FORTY-FOUR

Lash took a shower. After he brushed his teeth, he gargled generously with mouthwash. He even put on a tie when he got dressed.

He took a cab to the hospital.

Entering the hospital, he tried to appear confident as he approached the front desk.

"Can I help you?" the nurse there asked.

"I'm here to see Miranda Jameson," Lash said. "I'm her brother, Paul."

The nurse looked down at an open schedule book on the desk in front of her. She ran a finger down the page.

"I'm sorry," the woman said, looking back up at him. "But she isn't seeing any visitors at this time."

He recognized her voice then, from the phone call.

He tried to smile. "Are you sure about that? I mean, I came all the way out from Los Angeles this morning. Our parents are really worried. They asked me to check up on her."

"I'm sorry," the nurse said, sounding truly sorry. "But those are the rules."

"Can I at least ask why she was admitted?"

"I am not at liberty to discuss the case."

"I'm her brother, for Christ's sake," Lash said. Not that it seemed to be helping. "This whole thing is so shrouded in mystery that it has me scared. Is my baby sister going to die?"

He tried his best to sound very concerned, which wasn't difficult. The nurse reacted to the tone of his voice.

She looked around and beckoned him to come closer. Which he did.

"I suppose it could be life-threatening if she doesn't take care of herself," the nurse said. "If she doesn't alter her behavior."

"What is it?" he asked.

"Bulimia," the nurse said. "I think her esophagus was in pretty bad shape, but we can keep her stabilized here. She checked herself in yesterday afternoon, though, which is a good sign. It could get very serious if she gets worse."

How could she have gotten so ill since the last time I saw her? Lash wondered.

"Oh my God," Lash said. "Are you sure I can't just stick my head in and make sure she's okay? The folks would get really frazzled if I didn't have any news for them. If I didn't see her condition with my own eyes."

The nurse was hesitant.

"I swear, I'll be discreet."

"Okay," the nurse said. "She's in room 212. But don't stay too long."

"Thank you."

"Someone may try to stop you," the nurse said. "But explain that you spoke to me. I'm Nurse Camberone."

"I really want to thank you for this."

The nurse was in her late forties. She nodded and smiled. He could tell she was attracted to him, and that helped get the information.

Lash walked down the hall to the elevators. There were other people waiting to get on, and he blended in with them.

He got off on the second floor. The halls were full of people. People talking. Old people moving around with walkers. People overdressed and leaning against walls, waiting.

No one noticed him.

Lash was unhindered as he prowled the halls, looking for room 212. When he found it, he stopped outside the door and took a deep breath.

He went inside and stood just inside the doorway.

Miranda was lying in bed, watching television. She didn't seem to notice him at first. Then, she just stared at him. As he got closer, she seemed dismayed to see him.

"Hi," he said. "I was really worried about you. Why didn't you let me know where you were?"

"Didn't you get my note?" she asked. Her voice sounded horrible.

"Yeah, I got it," he said. "But I had no idea why you wrote it. Why you left. I didn't know you were coming here."

"I admitted myself," she told him. It was obvious that it hurt for her to talk. "I kept throwing up, even when there was nothing inside me. I couldn't stop."

"How are you now?" he asked.

"Better," she said. She was obviously uncomfortable, seeing him here. "I stopped at least. How did you know I was here?"

"I have my ways," he said, trying to dismiss it, but ending up sounding more mysterious.

"Listen," she said. "I meant what I wrote. What we had didn't work out. It's over."

"You're just feeling awful," he said. "We can talk about it when you're better."

"No," she said. She was very serious. "We're through. I don't want to talk about this. I shouldn't be talking at all. It hurts. You have to go."

"What did I do?" he asked. "What made you want to leave me?"

"I don't want to talk about this."

"I want to talk about it," he said. "I want to understand what went wrong."

"Please, Lash. Go away."

It reminded him of his conversation with Lizzie. But that was wrong. Lizzie was borderline psychotic. He was just someone who wanted answers to his questions.

She had her hand on the button to call the nurse, threatening to push it.

"Hey, you don't have to do that," he said. "I'm no threat to you. Why don't you just tell me what I did wrong? You actually seem angry at me. Tell me why."

"Please," she said.

A nurse entered the room. She must have pressed the button after all.

"What's going on here?" she asked.

"I would like this man to leave," Miranda said.

"Look, do you want me to tell your family you're okay?" Lash asked. "I'll call them if you want me to."

"I already spoke to them," Miranda said. "Please don't bother them. Please don't bother anyone I know. The letter I left you said all I wanted to say." She started to cry.

"No," he said. "It doesn't make sense. I don't understand any of this."

"You really should not be talking in your condition," the nurse said sternly to Miranda. "You're not even supposed to have visitors yet."

She turned her attention to Lash. "You're going to have to leave, sir. Miss Jameson is not allowed to have visitors right now."

The nurse grabbed his elbow.

"Let go of me," Lash said.

"You have to leave, sir."

"Let go of my arm, you bitch!" Lash shouted at her.

"I'll have to call security," the nurse said to Miranda, and left the room.

"Can't you just tell me why?" Lash asked. "What did I do?"

"It just didn't work," Miranda said. "Don't make a scene. Just leave, please."

The nurse came back in with a large man dressed in a white uniform.

"Is there a problem in here?" the man asked.

"I was just leaving," Lash said.

"Make it fast," the man said. "Or I'll *throw* you out."

Lash looked over at Miranda one last time. She had her head down, avoiding him.

He left.

"And don't come back," the nurse called out after him, following him out into the hall.

"Don't worry, I won't," Lash said.

The man walked behind him, down the hall, making sure that he got on the elevator.

He looked back. The nurse was talking on the phone.

The elevator opened. He went inside. The man followed on board and pressed the lobby button.

Lash just stood there, staring straight ahead at the elevator doors until they opened. Then he got out and went to the doors that led outside.

The man followed him all the way out and stood outside, watching him as he walked away.

CHAPTER FORTY-FIVE

As he approached his apartment building, Lash passed a group of children eating ice cream cones on a street corner. There was a chill in the air, and they were shivering.

As he climbed the steps to the front door, he felt a shiver himself.

He opened the door and went up the stairs to his apartment. Outside his door, as he went through his key ring until he isolated the right key, he heard his phone ringing inside. He got the door open and ran to answer it.

"Yeah," he said.

"Lash? It's Lizzie."

"Oh," he said, hearing the disappointment in his voice, and knowing that she heard it too.

"Did you see Miranda?" she asked.

"Yeah, I did."

"So," she said, then waited a moment. "Was I right?"

"Yeah," he said. "You were right. They weren't allowing any visitors, and I'm surprised I got in to see her, but I did."

"Well," she said. "Were you able to work things out?"

"How did you know she was there?"

"I always thought she looked malnourished," Lizzie said. "The hospitals were the first things I checked. It just so happened I had a friend in the know."

"What do you mean malnourished?" Lash asked. "And when did you meet her? I never introduced you."

"I drove by a few times and saw her with you," Lizzie said. "What's the big deal?"

"What, were you spying on us?"

"Listen, I didn't help you to put up with these accusations," she said. "Sometimes I drive by that area, and I saw the two of you together. That's all."

"Well," he said. "It doesn't matter now, anyway."

"Did you two work things out?"

"I really don't want to go into it right now," Lash said. "I've got things to do."

"Please, just tell me," she said. "Did my information help?"

"It might be a lost cause," Lash said. "I don't know, yet. I really have to go."

"Okay," she said. She wanted so badly to keep him on the phone. Keep him talking. "But, if you need anyone to talk to, give me a call. Okay? Anytime."

"Yeah, sure."

"Bye," she said, and hung up first. She couldn't bear to hear him hang up on her.

He waited for the dial tone and listened to it for a minute before he put the phone down.

He turned and faced the door. He had left it open, in his haste to answer the phone. He went over to it now and closed it. Locked it.

Then Lash walked over to the television and turned it on.

There was a human face on the screen, close up, and it was twisted and lacerated. The eyes wide and glassy, and the person could have been dead. It looked like the result of an accident. The sound was off.

He walked away, to the middle of the room, then turned and looked at that face again.

It seemed frozen in time. The lack of sound only accentuated this.

Then, the scene changed. Two men were sitting on black leather chairs in a studio. They appeared to be having a heated argument.

Lash went to the kitchen and found two beer bottles in the refrigerator. He opened them both and brought them back into the living room with him.

He sat down in front of the television and grabbed the remote. He held the two bottlenecks in one hand and turned up the sound with the other.

He caught the last shouts of the men in the studio. Their sounds were like loud grunts. Incoherent. Then, the scene changed again, to a commercial.

A woman's hand held a glass of red-colored liquid. Water with food coloring. She poured the liquid onto a tampon.

A woman's voice-over said, "See, this brand doesn't absorb enough."

Lash took turns swigging from each bottle.

He wondered what Cindy was doing.

CHAPTER FORTY-SIX

L ash stood in the dimly lit hallway, listening to the music that was coming through the door. There was a little peephole in the door, and he knew someone was looking out at him. He could feel it.

The door opened. The music got louder. He could hear Jim Morrison singing about the end.

"Hi," Lash said.

Dasko took off his glasses and wiped one of his eyes. "Is it really you, Lash? Long time, no see," he said. "I was beginning to wonder if maybe you'd dropped off the face of the Earth."

"I know," Lash said. "Things have been kind of crazy, lately."

It had been a long time since Lash had visited any of his male friends. It was not like he had a lot of them, but he used to hang out with Dasko all the time. He felt bad that he had been neglecting the guy. They hadn't seen each other in a couple of months.

"Well, you might as well come in," Dasko said. "Want something to drink?"

"What do you think?" Lash said, and then smiled.

"All I've got is beer."

"I brought a present," Lash said, handing him a bag with a fifth of bourbon inside.

"Very nice."

They'd been shouting over the music. Dasko went over and turned down the stereo. Then he disappeared for a few minutes. Lash wandered into the living room.

There was an easel in one corner of the room. On it was a canvas. A painting in progress. It was the close-up of a human face. The face was so close that it was hard to determine whether it was male or female. The face was smeared with red paint.

"What's it called?" Lash asked, motioning to the painting.

Dasko was coming back into the room with two glasses and two bottles of beer. He took the bourbon out of the bag and filled the glasses, then he popped open the beer chasers.

"Face Smeared with Blood," Dasko said, then laughed. "I don't know. Do you like it?"

"Sure," Lash said. "I kind of miss being able to watch an artist at work."

"Well, it's not like you're banished from coming here," Dasko said. Then, "Things have been kind of solitary around here for a while now. Sissy left about a month ago."

"I'm sorry," Lash said. "I had heard rumors. Of course, it wouldn't have been all that hard to just call and ask you myself. I've been meaning to come over for a visit, but I guess I've been caught up in my own little soap opera lately."

"You still with Miranda?" Dasko asked. He scratched at his thick, unkempt beard.

He used to always keep himself so trim. So well-manicured. But he had obviously let himself go since Sissy left.

"Miranda left, too," Lash said. "But I have no idea why. We both had our own apartments for a long time, and she used to bug me about moving in with me. So she finally does it, finally moves in, and then a few weeks later, she just takes off. It's got me dumbfounded."

"What was it, another man?" Dasko asked. "Or did you have another woman on the side that she caught wind of?"

"Neither," Lash said. "I mean, I don't think so. It really makes no sense to me. We were doing so well, and then, without warning, it just fell apart."

"Where is she now?"

"In the hospital," Lash said. "She had herself admitted. Turns out that she was bulimic."

"I always thought she was kind of skinny," Dasko said. "The few times I saw her. But I thought I was being too judgmental. If she's in the hospital, then that just means she's gone temporarily, right?"

"No."

"What do you mean? Did you go visit her?"

"Yeah, I went, but she made it very clear she didn't want me there. Besides, before she left me, she wrote a note. It spelled things out. It was over between us. I just have no idea *why*, that's all. She said that her health problems had nothing to do with the breakup, but she wouldn't articulate the reason. She wouldn't clear up the mystery."

"Think about it," Dasko said. "You must have done something to trigger it."

"I have to admit to you, I've been getting kind of involved with someone else, but Miranda couldn't have known anything about that. In fact, it happened so recently, and so fast, that I've barely had time to let it sink in myself."

"Is it a client of yours?" Dasko asked.

Lash had sat down on a chair near the painting. Dasko stood in the shadows.

"Yeah," Lash said. "I've known her awhile, but only recently has she let me know that she's interested. I guess I've been interested since we first met, but we move in different worlds, so I never really thought much about it. When she came on to me, though, I found it hard to resist."

"I wish I had your talents," Dasko said. "I'd have me a pretty rich patron by now."

"But this thing between us only just started. It caught me completely off-guard. There's no way Miranda could have found out about it."

"If she hadn't left you, what would have happened with this client of yours?" Dasko asked. "Would it have gotten serious?"

"I don't know," Lash said. "It would have gotten *complicated*; I know that much. This client really turns me on. Her name is Cindy, and there is this strong sexual thing there. I've never felt such a magnetic pull. But I really cared about Miranda. I still do. When she left, it hurt me more than I thought it would. I had a real bad reaction to it. I would have ended the thing with Cindy, eventually. I wanted something lasting with Miranda, or at least I thought I did. Now, I'm not sure about anything."

"So you're giving up on Miranda," Dasko said.

"It looks like she's given up on me."

"What about Lizzie?"

"What about her?"

"She still a pain in the ass?"

"She's always nearby," Lash said. "If that's what you mean. I think she's been spying on me. Since the divorce, I feel like I'm walking on eggs whenever I see her. I have told her to fuck off, but she won't take it seriously. When I confront her, she has this way of disarming me. It's hard to explain, really. I don't love her anymore, in fact, I resent the way she intrudes on my life. But I can't stay mad at her, and I can't get rid of her. I want to, but something won't let me cut it off at the neck."

"She has a hold on you," Dasko said. "She always did. A chokehold of guilt. We've talked about this before. Nothing seems to have changed."

"No," Lash said. "Not really."

"So here we are, two lonely jerk-offs," Dasko said. "Welcome to the club."

Lash drained his glass, then the bottle of beer.

"Want another setup?"

"Sure."

Dasko retreated into the shadows. Lash got up and followed him.

"It's getting dark," Lash said. "Why don't you turn on the lights?"

"Naw, I like it this way."

Dasko opened the refrigerator, and the light inside illuminated the kitchen. He pulled out two fresh bottles and handed one to Lash. Then he filled the glasses with bourbon again "So, is it possible that Lizzie could have something to do with Miranda leaving you?"

"What do you mean?"

"Could she have said something?" Dasko said. "Maybe she went behind your back. Told Miranda stuff. Maybe made her think you were still seeing her on the side. You know. I wouldn't put it past her to try to break the two of you up. Not the Lizzie I know."

"I never thought of that."

"I guess it would be hard to find out," Dasko said. "If

Miranda won't talk to you. And you know Lizzie would never admit it. But as you also know, she can be convincing when she wants to be. She's one spooky broad."

"I don't think she did it," Lash said, but down deep he couldn't be sure. It wasn't so far-fetched, after all. He knew she couldn't stand to see another woman taking up his time. And she was the only one who knew exactly where Miranda was. What was *that* about?

He had made her agree to stay away. He had told her that things were serious between him and Miranda. But maybe Lizzie's jealousy was just too strong. It wouldn't surprise him at all.

"Well, it's just an idea," Dasko said. "You said you had no idea why Miranda left. I was just trying to create a scenario that might explain it."

"Dasko, something else happened recently," Lash said. "Something else that bothered me in the worst way."

"Well?"

"I went to see a client of mine," Lash said. "A man named Antony. I think I'd mentioned him before."

"The rich guy," Dasko said. "The one Lizzie whored you out to way back when. Yeah, I remember."

"He was a nice guy," Lash said. "Really, he was. He was my oldest client."

"Yeah."

"I went to see him one night, and he had killed himself. He was hanging by a rope from the ceiling."

"Oh, man!"

"But that's not what freaked me out," Lash said. "I wanted to run away when I saw it. But something stopped me. I fell to the floor and started rolling."

"You mean like when you intensify people's orgasms?"

"Yeah, except, it was like I was intensifying the death that was in that room. Channeling it. Sucking it in."

"Sounds pretty weird."

"I'd never experienced anything like that before," Lash said. "It was totally out of my control. I don't know how I stopped. It was all out of my hands."

Dasko grunted.

"Ever since then, there have been times when I've felt really weird," Lash said. "There have been hallucinations. They don't last long, and it's not like I'm losing my mind or anything. But it's very disturbing."

"I guess it would be," Dasko said. He took a pull from his beer. "Hey, did you ever tell Miranda what you did for a living?"

"Yeah, eventually," Lash said. "She seemed to have a problem with that. She wanted me to stop doing it, and find a *real* job, but I refused. No way I'm going back to that shit. Maybe that had something to do with why she left."

"It's possible," Dasko said. "I guess you could analyze all this to death and find a dozen reasons why she might have left you. I think the best thing would be just to get your mind off it for a while. You're thinking yourself into a dead end."

They sat there, drinking, illuminated by the refrigerator light. Dasko had left the door open.

"So, how have you been since Sissy left?" Lash asked. "How long were you together? Five years?"

"Six," Dasko said. "On and off. This was the last time, though. She won't be coming back. But I'll tell you, since she left, I've had this incredible wave of creativity. I haven't stopped for a minute. It's like she gave me a jump-start by taking off on me."

"Really?"

"Yeah," Dasko said. "What have you got planned for tonight? It's a Saturday night, after all."

"Nothing," Lash said. "That's why I'm here."

Dasko scowled at him. Then they both laughed.

"How's about we do what we did in the good old days," Dasko suggested. "We can head out for some drinks and then hit a club."

"Who's playing?"

"Moe's band is over the Screen Door," Dasko said. "And I know he would love to see you. Besides, he can get us some free drinks."

"Sounds good to me," Lash said.

"Let me get dressed," Dasko said. He was wearing denim overalls covered with paint.

"Yeah, sure."

Dasko walked out of the kitchen. Lash followed. He finally turned on a light in his bedroom and went looking for clothes to change into.

"It sure has been a long time," Dasko said. "I almost missed you. We sure used to have a lot of laughs together."

"Why did Sissy leave, anyhow?"

"I have to admit it. Things got ugly toward the end there. I smacked her around one night. It was stupid, but it was kind of an explosive night. We were both shouting and throwing things. We'd been drinking and it was the worst fight we ever had. Well, at one point she hit me in the eye, and I kind of freaked out. When it was over, we both knew it was time to end things."

"I bet she decked you," Lash said, and laughed.

Dasko didn't smile. "She got in some good ones. But I really hurt her. Could have killed her if I didn't stop myself. If I didn't realize what was happening. It was like coming out of a nightmare, you know."

He slipped the shoulder straps of his overalls off and pulled the top part down. There were scars on his chest. Red slashes. One split a nipple in half.

"You weren't exaggerating, were you?" Lash asked.

"We got sick of each other," Dasko said. "We should have ended it sooner. It's too bad it came down to violence before we realized it."

"Did anyone call the cops."

"In this neighborhood? No. No cops. We could have murdered each other and there wouldn't have been a peep."

"It's tough to make things work," Lash said.

"Yeah, but you have to be able to tell when it's over," Dasko said. "That's my problem. I'm too dumb to figure that out. Well, not anymore."

He grabbed his beer bottle and went to the bathroom. He turned on the shower. Lash leaned against the wall in the hallway.

"So you're still rolling around on the floor for a living, huh?" Dasko asked.

"Yeah," Lash said. "It sounds crazy, but it pays good. I've got a real nice nest egg because of it."

"Nest egg?" Dasko asked. "What are you going to do with it?"

"How the fuck should I know?" Lash asked.

Then he thought about it.

"Maybe someday I'll just go away somewhere. Some place far away. And I'll start all over again."

"Sounds good," Dasko said. "Sounds really good. I wish to God I could start over again."

And it *did* sound good. Somehow, Lash had never thought of it until tonight.

"I won't be long," Dasko said, closing the bathroom door. "As soon I get ready, we can head out."

CHAPTER FORTY-SEVEN

They were back in Dasko's apartment. Lash faintly remembered going out to a club. People dancing. More drinking. And then a girl. Looked like a college kid. She looked Indian, maybe. Dasko knew her from when he used to teach night classes. She seemed very friendly to him, and it was clear they had had some kind of relationship before.

Somehow, they ended up back here. The girl was topless. She had the smallest tits he had ever seen and she was doing some kind of crazy dance to a song on the radio. Heavy synthesizers. Dasko had his shirt off and was trying to imitate her. Lash was on the bed. They were all laughing.

Then they stopped dancing and Dasko grabbed her arm and pulled her onto the bed. He was telling Lash that she gave the most amazing blowjobs, and she was unzipping his pants.

Lash was drinking from a glass of gin as she blew him, and then he pushed her away. He didn't want to come that way, and Dasko, who had been watching the whole time less than three feet away, made her stand up. He pulled her jeans and underwear down, and he was doing her from behind.

The next thing he knew, Dasko was down on the bed, and he was fucking her in the ass. She was on top, facing Lash, and he went to her. He pulled off his shorts and crawled to where she was and he rubbed her vagina. He slipped a few fingers in, and she was going wild. It was so wet. Then he maneuvered himself and slipped his cock inside her.

It was the first time he had ever double-teamed a girl, and it was an odd sensation. He could feel Dasko moving around inside her. The skin between them was thinner than he thought. He had seen double penetration in porno movies lots of times, but he had never done anything like this in real life before. And Dasko, hidden beneath the girl, was laughing.

They were both fucking her now and she was squealing like a pig. And Lash thought it was interesting to fuck like a normal person, without the rolling around on the ground. Sure he had tried to keep it normal with Miranda, too, but this was the first time since she broke things off, and it all felt so dirty, so forbidden, and the girl had such a bright young face, grinning ear to ear as she came.

And Lash came, too, and the three of them got tangled up together as they took turns coming and then Lash fell off the bed and onto the floor.

CHAPTER FORTY-EIGHT

Lash opened his eyes and found himself on a cold floor in a dark room. His head ached.

He stood up, slowly, and heard empty beer bottles roll across the floor.

Lash moved toward the wall; his hands stretched out to feel it. He stumbled against a light switch and flicked it on.

He was still in Dasko's apartment. He had been sleeping on the living room floor. Dark brown, hardwood floor. There were beer bottles everywhere. And he looked down at himself. He was wearing a girl's panties. They were too small and stretched really tight on his body. He was surprised. They looked normal enough, but he thought all young girls these days wore thongs.

Lash went over to a window. He pulled the shade aside and looked outside. The sun was beginning to rise.

He let the shade drop back into place and wandered around the apartment. There was a sound that guided him. Dasko's snoring. The door to Dasko's bedroom was open, and Dasko was sprawled across his bed, naked and sleeping soundly. The girl was nowhere in sight. She must have split.

Lash stood in the doorway and watched his friend sleep.

Then, he wandered around the place, finding his clothes, making sure that he had his wallet and keys. And then he left the apartment.

Out in the dimly lit hallway, he felt the throbbing in his head getting worse.

When he got outside, he walked for about a block, when he found a coffee shop. There weren't many people there yet, but it would be filling up soon. He took a seat and the far end of the counter. Coffee was placed in front of him, almost immediately, and he took a sip.

"What day is it?" he asked the waitress, the next time she came near.

"Monday morning," she said. "You're having a rough time of it, huh?"

"I'll live," Lash said, realizing that there was a whole day he couldn't account for.

When he finished the coffee, and a refill, he put some change down on the counter and headed for home.

CHAPTER FORTY-NINE

Lash didn't even realize where he was, until he opened the door to the apartment. It wasn't his place, it was Miranda's.

His head was still throbbing, but he knew that he didn't mean to come here. He didn't belong here. This wasn't his space. It was hers. He was an invader.

Lash turned and closed the door behind him. He did it softly, quietly. He turned on the lights, knowing before they came on that the place was empty.

Completely empty.

All her things were gone. Her clothes, her books, her furniture. Everything. Any sign that she had once lived here was gone. He did not have to go from room to room to confirm this, but he did it anyway. He opened the closets and scanned the floors, trying to find some clue that she had been here. Something he could remember her by.

Inside of a cabinet in the kitchen, he found a balled-up photograph. He flattened it out. It was of him and Miranda. They were laughing. Looking at it, he was sure that it had been left there for him to find. That it had been left there on purpose.

He put it in his pocket.

He stood in the kitchen, leaning over the sink, holding on to the edges, closing his eyes to try to relieve the pain of his hangover. He felt as if he would cry.

But he didn't.

It was over. He realized that now. She had gone away. She would never come back to him.

Lash knew that if he went back to the hospital, if he could somehow get back into her room, he would find that she was no longer there, either.

Chances were slim that she was even in the same state.

He wondered if she had moved the stuff out herself. Probably not. She wouldn't have been strong enough, so soon after her illness. He tried to think of people who might have moved things for her. Friends, perhaps. Or relatives he had never met. It really didn't matter.

He felt a wave of grief coming over him, but it died in its tracks, before he could be overcome by it.

Instead, he felt nothing. Numb.

Lash opened his eyes and looked around the kitchen where she would sometimes cook for him when they had first started dating. It was just some meaningless place now. Empty.

There was no reason to stay here. It meant nothing to him now.

He left the apartment, locking the door behind him.

CHAPTER FIFTY

Lash turned the key in his door and went inside. He felt like a sleepwalker trying to find a door in a dream.

As soon as he closed the door, he knew that he wasn't alone.

He put the chain lock on and walked to his bedroom. Someone was sleeping in his bed. And it wasn't Goldilocks.

It was Lizzie.

As he stood over the bed, staring down at her, she stirred as if on cue.

She was wrapped in his sheet, and, as she squirmed, he could see that she was naked.

"Lash?" she said softly, trying to sit up. "Lash, is that you?"

"Yeah, it's me," he said. "What the fuck are you doing here?"

"I was worried," she said, rubbing her eyes. "I thought you'd never come back."

"You didn't hear me, did you?" he asked. "I want to know what you're doing here, in my bed."

"I was waiting for you," she said, looking up at him. The sheet slipped from her and she made no attempt to cover her breasts. "Waiting for you to come back."

"Why? You don't live here. And I don't want you here."

"Don't say that," she said, softly. Then, louder, "Don't say that anymore!"

"Get dressed," he told her. "Get dressed and go back to your own bed."

He left the room and went to the kitchen. On the way, he stopped at the phone. He had a few messages. He poured himself some milk and tossed down some aspirin. He pushed the "play" button on his machine.

The first message was from Dasko. Actually, it was from

him and Dasko. Both of them were singing drunkenly. Lash did not remember doing it, but there were a lot of things he didn't remember about the weekend. Listening to the loud, off-key voices singing made Lash's head start throbbing again, so he pressed the "delete" button.

He wondered how bad Dasko would feel when he woke up.

He hoped the next message would be from Cindy, but it wasn't. It was one of his other clients, reminding him of an appointment they had later that day. He was in no mood to go, but it was too late to cancel now.

He had to do a few things first, though.

First, he had to get rid of Lizzie.

As he turned to go back to the bedroom, he saw that Lizzie was walking toward him. She hadn't put her clothes on.

"Get dressed," he told her. "I want to be alone."

"I just woke up," she said. She was pleading, now. "Don't throw me out like this."

"I'm serious," he said. "I want you to leave."

How many times had he said that to her in his lifetime?

She reacted like she did to the other times he had said it. She ignored him. She came closer and tried to put her arms around him.

He pushed her away.

"I know you're upset about Miranda," Lizzie said. "And I want to help you."

"I don't need any help," he told her. "How long have you been here, anyway?"

"Not long," she said, and he knew she was lying. She pursed her lips and then she said, "Not long at all. Really."

"You were here long enough to sleep over. I thought I told you to give me your key back."

She didn't say anything in response.

"Listen, I don't care how long you've been here. The point is that you're here. And I don't want you here. So, just get your things together and leave."

Lash walked past her, to the bedroom. He sat down on the bed and pressed the cold glass of milk to his temple. It seemed to help a little.

Lizzie stood in the doorway, watching him.

"You don't want me to leave," she said, softly. She sounded so sure of herself. "I know you don't."

He was tired of arguing with her. This wouldn't go anywhere if he continued to talk to her. He drank the milk and put the glass on his night table. Then he stretched on the bed and covered his head with a pillow.

She stood, watching him in silence. After a while, she crawled into the bed beside him and embraced him tightly.

He didn't bother to push her away.

CHAPTER FIFTY-ONE

Lash woke in a haze sometime later. His pants were off, and Lizzie was alternately fondling his cock and putting it in her mouth.

His first instinct was to push her away, but he didn't do that. Instead, he let the pillow fall to one side and tilted his head to watch her.

She gave no indication that she was aware that he was watching her, but he knew that she felt his eyes on her.

When she got him good and hard, she got on top of him, and slid him inside her.

He closed his eyes and let the sensations wash over him. His headache was gone and he was feeling better. No nausea, no aches and pains.

Lizzie moved on top of him. She was very wet, like she had been anticipating this for a long time.

He opened his eyes.

She winked at him.

It was then that he felt something else. It was like a mouth was sucking on his penis, but it couldn't be. Lizzie was fucking him. But he could feel that mouth, *too*.

It was the strangest thing he had ever felt, but it was damned pleasurable.

The feeling was so intense that the orgasm happened without warning. He didn't even try to delay it. He just closed his eyes and enjoyed it.

When she was done, Lizzie slid off him and went to the bathroom.

Lash stayed very still, enjoying the aftershocks. He was

actually tingling. And he waited a bit before he turned to look at the clock on the night table.

He had to start getting ready for his appointment.

Lash sat up slowly and waited for the sound of the shower running. Lizzie always took a shower right after sex.

Lash pulled his shirt off and wiped his cock with some tissues. Then he looked for some fresh clothes to wear.

When he picked out what he wanted, he went into the bathroom.

"I've got to see a client soon," he shouted. "I'm in a rush."

"You should have told me," she said. "We could have taken a shower together. Like old times."

He stood there, watching as she toweled herself dry.

"We can still take a shower together, if you want," she said, and smiled at him.

"I don't have time," he said.

She had left the water running for him, and he got inside the shower stall. He lathered himself up. There were bruises on his body he didn't remember having. From his wild weekend with Dasko.

He got dressed and went out into the living room. He could smell the aroma of bacon cooking.

"I didn't know I had any bacon," he said, entering the kitchen. Lizzie was wearing his old bathrobe, and her wet hair hung to her shoulders.

"You didn't," she said, not turning around from where she stood, at the stove. "I bought some on my way over last night. Some eggs, too."

"Like you knew you'd be staying until morning."

"I wanted to be prepared, that's all," she said, sounding defensive.

He was tempted to start an argument with her again, but stopped himself.

"I know how much you love bacon," she said.

"Don't you work anymore?" he asked her. "I mean, it's the middle of the day on a Monday."

"I took the day off," she said. "They won't miss me."

"I have to leave soon," he said. "I suggest you go home."

She handed him a plate of fried eggs and bacon. "Let me put some toast on."

"Did you hear what I said?"

She ignored him and pressed down the lever on the toaster.

"You'd better start eating before it gets cold," she told him.

He knew he wouldn't press the point. Not after the way she woke him up. Between the incredible sex, and now, bacon cooked just the way he liked it, soft and moist, he felt like he had to give her a break, just this once.

He went out into the living room and sat down at the coffee table. He started eating. She came out with a plate of buttered toast and a fresh glass of milk.

He didn't say another word as he ate.

CHAPTER FIFTY-TWO

The subway stop was across the street from the hotel, and Lash looked up at the fifth-floor windows, trying to guess which one his client was in.

He crossed the street, and, once inside, got in the elevator. As it rose, he watched the numbers take turns lighting up.

On the fifth floor, he stepped out into a long, empty corridor. Downstairs, he had seen a couple of people in uniform milling around in the lobby. But up here, the place seemed devoid of life.

He walked down the hall to the right room and knocked on the door.

The door opened, and he was beckoned inside.

The client was a large man, more than a head taller than Lash, and slightly overweight for his height. His hair was closely cropped. His name was Mr. Anaram.

"Good to see you," he said to Lash.

It had been a couple of months since they'd last seen each other. Lash found himself thinking about how he saw some of his older clients less and less over the years. Antony had been his only constant. He wondered why this was. And he decided it was time he looked for more new clients.

Mr. Anaram was wearing a bathrobe and, for a moment, it made Lash think of Lizzie. He wasn't sure why.

There was a big-screen television against one wall. On it, gangsters were shooting one another in the middle of a busy street.

Mr. Anaram was another of those faceless clients he had originally met through Lizzie, when she had been involved in his "career."

The man sat down on a long, plush sofa. It was only other piece of furniture in the room, except for the television. Sitting down, the man's robe opened, and Lash could see he was naked underneath.

There was an envelope on the sofa, and a remote control. The man sighed and held the envelope out for Lash. Lash took it and put it in his pocket.

"Is the room big enough?" Anaram asked.

Lash nodded his head and removed his clothes and folded them. He did it slowly. The man watched him undress. He sighed every now and then, and it made Lash nervous.

He kept his underwear on and got down on the carpet.

There was a click. The gangster movie on the television screen was replaced with a porno film. A woman was sucking on a man's cock. She looked like she was really enjoying it.

From where he lay, Lash could not see the man on the sofa, but he knew that the man was fondling himself.

Lash looked over at the television screen. The woman was on all fours, getting fucked by a faceless man. She was grunting and squirming.

Lash closed his eyes. And slowly moved back and forth.

He heard moans. Some of them came from Anaram, but those were more like grunts and hisses. The actual, female moans came from the screen. And for some reason, they made Lash think of what had happened earlier in the day with Lizzie. How amazing it had felt. He couldn't remember her doing it like that before.

He heard new noises, coming from the other side of the wall, and it sounded like other people were fucking in the room next door, and because the walls were so thin, what he was doing was affecting them, too.

It took him a little longer than usual to go into his trance. His bruises hurt when he rolled on them. But eventually he could feel the numbness spreading through his body.

When Lash came out of his trance, he was stretched out on the carpet, wet with sweat. A news show was on the television screen. The porno movie had finished.

Mr. Anaram was quiet.

Lash felt moisture on his forehead and touched it with his hand. It was sticky and mostly dried. Some of the man's ejaculate must have reached him.

Lash stood up and glanced at his client. Anaram had his head back and seemed to be staring up at the ceiling. He couldn't tell whether the man's eyes were open or closed. The man's genitals were wet with semen.

Lash wandered around until he found a bathroom. He washed his hands and then wiped his forehead with a wet cloth.

When he left, the man was still on the sofa, head tilted back. Lash couldn't tell if he was breathing or not. He didn't hear any sounds.

"Are you okay?" he asked.

Anaram did not move, but he couldn't be dead. If he was, Lash would probably be back down on the floor, sucked into another trance beyond his control.

But he could feel himself shaking. If Anaram wasn't dead, maybe he was on the verge of death. Whether or not Lash was responsible, he did not want to stay here any longer. He didn't want to go close enough to check for a pulse or for a heartbeat. He didn't want to touch the guy.

He stared at the big man as he got dressed. Then he left, wondering if he should call for an ambulance, but deciding not to.

Out in the hall, waiting for the elevator to stop on his floor, Lash could feel the shaking getting worse. He almost took the stairs down, just to get out of this place quickly, when the elevator finally opened. He stepped inside.

Lash nervously brushed his forehead with the tips of his fingers.

CHAPTER FIFTY-THREE

When Lash got back to his apartment, Lizzie was still there, just as he knew she would be.

He went straight to the bathroom without talking to her. He ran the water, wet a face cloth, and dabbed at his forehead. He stared at himself in the mirror over the sink, as if he expected to see someone else there.

Lizzie stood in the doorway and watched him. He could see her in the mirror. She was dressed now. Wearing a bright red blouse and blue jeans. She looked good and it reminded him of when they first met and were addicted to each other's bodies. While he had moved on, she still seemed to have that addiction.

"How did it go?" she asked.

"How did *what* go?"

"The job," she said. "What else? How did it go?"

"They're all about the same."

"Are you free for the rest of the day?"

"Why?"

"Well, I thought maybe we could do something. Together."

"No, thanks," Lash said.

He went over to the shower and turned on the water.

"Why not?" she asked. "How about a movie? I know you love movies. There must be something you want to see."

"I think you're putting too much emphasis on what happened this morning," Lash said. "Not a hell of a lot has changed between us. I still don't want you staying here. I want my space."

"But Miranda's out of the picture now."

He wanted to ask Lizzie if she had anything to do with Miranda's leaving, but he didn't. If she was responsible, she would never admit it.

"Even if she is, I lived alone a long time before she moved in here. In fact, I lived alone a long time before I ever met her, after you and I got divorced. I'm the kind of guy who likes to have his own place, his own territory. You know that. I think you're kidding yourself if you think we can rekindle some kind of romance between us."

"So, you're saying that this morning didn't mean anything at all?" Lizzie asked him.

"We both enjoyed it, okay? I'll admit that. But I don't want you to think I'm interested in some kind of relationship with you again. I don't need any extra complications in my life."

Lizzie pouted. He used to find that sexy. He still did, though he wouldn't admit it now.

"I have to take a shower," Lash said.

He gently pushed her out of the way and closed the bathroom door. He locked it. Then he got undressed and got into the shower.

When he was done, he opened the bathroom door a crack and looked outside. Lizzie was not waiting outside the door. He ran across the hall, into the bedroom, and got fresh clothes.

The apartment was quiet. Maybe she had left.

When he walked into the living room, he found Lizzie stretched out on the sofa, drinking a glass of wine.

"You still here?"

"Yes, I'm still here."

"You must be hard of hearing."

"Have some wine," she said. "It would do you a world of good. To relax."

He ignored her. "Look, are you going to leave, or do I have to make you?"

"Is that a threat?"

"I told you, I'd like some time to think. Is that a crime?"

"Like I said, you need to relax."

"That's right."

"Well, you seemed pretty relaxed this morning, when I was fucking you."

"I don't want to talk about this anymore."

"Let's do it again," she said. "I want to."

"This isn't about sex," he said. "This is about my sanity. I want you out of here."

"So you keep telling me," she said. "But I think what you really need is someone to turn you on. To get you off. You need someone to help you forget your problems."

"You're not listening to a single fucking thing I'm saying, are you?"

"Maybe I'm not listening to you because it's all bullshit," Lizzie said. "Don't you find me attractive anymore? I used to really turn you on before. Remember?"

"You look fine," he said. "But this has nothing to do with that. What I don't like is the way you're dogging me. I can feel your breath down my neck all the time, and I don't like it. I need a break."

Lizzie finished her wine and put the glass down on the floor.

She got up and moved toward him.

"Fuck me."

"I don't want to give you any false hope," he said. "And I don't want to play these games anymore. I'm tired."

"Come on," she said, playfully. "Don't you want to?"

"It would just make things worse," he said. "You'll get more obsessive. You know you will. This is what ruined our marriage in the first place."

"What? The sex?" she asked. She smiled then, and almost laughed.

"No, this thing you have with me. This hang-up you have. You have this idea that we can just forget all the bad shit that's gone down between us and just fall in love all over again, like a prince and princess in some fucking fairy tale and live happily ever after. But you have to face reality. We're through. We've been through for a long time now."

"But we can still make love," she said. "What harm is there in that?"

She put her arms around him. He was very still. She could feel his tension.

"Please," he said.

"Take me," she told him. "I'm yours."

She licked his neck.

He closed his eyes and stood there as she undid his belt.

"Take me," she said. "Right here, on the floor."

She licked the inside of his thigh.

He got down on his knees beside her and grabbed her. They sprawled out across the floor, pulling each other's clothes off and fondling and kissing one another.

CHAPTER FIFTY-FOUR

Lash woke in the middle of the night, and Lizzie was unconscious on the bed beside him, her arms thrown across his chest. The bedroom was in disarray. Clothes were thrown about the room, as well as the blankets and sheets.

There were empty wine bottles on the floor, and the light was still on. He looked at the clock. It was quarter past midnight.

Gently, Lash disengaged himself from Lizzie's arms and got out of bed. He went to the bathroom and looked at himself in the mirror. Then he lifted the toilet seat and took a piss.

He must have had sex with Lizzie at least four times in the last eight hours. He even remembered rolling around on the floor for a while, while she touched herself, driving her crazy with passion.

He had no idea how she had been able to manipulate him into letting her stay, and how she had been able to excite him so strongly. During their lovemaking, he was once more amazed at the strange sensations he felt. It truly felt as if there was a mouth inside her, sucking him as she fucked him. It had to be some kind of trick, but she had never used it before, and no matter how hard he thought about it, he could not think of a logical explanation.

He went back to the bedroom and sat at the foot of the bed. There was a bottle by the bed with some wine left in it. He lifted it to his lips.

"Lash."

It was a soft voice. Muffled. He turned to look at Lizzie, but she was still out cold.

"Lash, I'm over here."

The voice, strangely enough, seemed to be coming near

Lizzie's legs. Her legs were spread apart as she slept, the sheets were on the floor, and Lash found his eyes focused between them. He saw something incredibly strange. Her vaginal lips were being pushed to the sides and what looked like a human tongue was sticking out of her.

Lizzie's lower abdomen was moving strangely, as if something was inside of her, moving around in there.

Lash put down the bottle and moved closer to where the tongue was. When he was close enough, it withdrew, back into Lizzie once more.

"Lash," the voice said, keeping the labia spread apart so it could speak to him.

"Come closer," the voice said, now that it had his attention. Something moved forward, toward him. A human mouth. Its lips were exposed, within Lizzie's vaginal lips.

"It's me," the mouth said.

"Who?" he whispered.

"Miranda."

"I'm going nuts," he whispered to himself.

"No, Lash," the mouth said. "It's really me."

The mouth moved back, and he could see something squirming around inside Lizzie's abdomen. It could have been a head. The mouth was replaced with an eye, looking straight out at him from Lizzie's gaping vagina. It was a bright blue eye, like one of Miranda's. The eye drew back again, and what he thought of as Miranda's head shifted around until he saw the mouth again.

"Lash, you have to get me out of here."

"What the hell are you doing in there?"

"I'm a captive," Miranda's mouth said. "Lizzie's keeping me a prisoner in here."

"How?" Lash asked. "None of this makes any sense."

"She wants you all to herself," the mouth said. "I don't know how she did this to me, but she did. And only you can get me out."

"How?" he wanted to know.

"Lash, you just have to get me out of here, somehow. I don't know how much longer I can last."

"How do I do it without waking Lizzie up?"

"Who cares about that?" the mouth asked. "Just get me out. *Cut* me out of here."

"*Cut* you out?"

"Like a baby, like a C-section," the mouth said. "You have to set me free."

Lizzie made a soft noise. It looked like she was going to move, but then she was very still again.

"I have to think about this," Lash said.

"Please, don't think too long," Miranda's mouth pleaded. "Only you can save me, Lash."

Lash moved away from Lizzie and stood up. He picked up the bottle with wine in it and left the room.

In the bathroom, he sat on the toilet seat and finished the bottle, thinking about what he had seen. There was no way in hell it could have been real. But he had seen it. And he had felt it. It had been Miranda's mouth that had been sucking on him when he had been fucking Lizzie. It all made sense now. He had witnessed Miranda with at least three of his senses: sight, sound, and touch. So she *had* to be real, didn't she? He finished the bottle of wine.

He went over to the mirror and touched his forehead. It seemed to be wet there, sticky. A fissure erupted there suddenly, causing him to pull his fingers away. It took shape as he watched, becoming a kind of vaginal opening, above his right eye. It quivered and seemed to be moving like a sideways mouth, but it made no sound.

Lash closed his eyes tightly and tried to clear his mind. When he opened his eyes, the vagina that had formed on his forehead was gone.

It was a hallucination.

Just like Miranda's mouth. That *couldn't* be real.

But he had felt it several times. When he had sex with Lizzie.

He went into the kitchen and got a fresh bottle of wine. Then he walked over to the television and turned it on.

There was an old horror movie on. A strange, octopus-like creature was pulling screaming people toward its vast, vagina-like mouth.

CHAPTER FIFTY-FIVE

Lash woke again around three in the morning. Lizzie was still asleep.

He moved slowly, carefully, so that he didn't disturb Lizzie. He put his head on the bed, between her legs. She always kicked the sheets off, and she always slept in the nude.

There was a flashlight that he had put under the bed the last time he had woken up. He had it on, and he focused its beam on Lizzie's sex.

Waiting for a sign.

Waiting for confirmation. For proof that what he had seen, had felt, was real.

It didn't take long. A tongue stuck out at him. He moved closer.

"Lash," a voice whispered. "Are you there?"

He had his head right near Lizzie's vagina. He aimed the beam of light.

"Miranda?" he whispered in answer.

"Come closer," the voice said.

Whatever was inside of Lizzie pushed her vaginal lips apart, and Lash could see Miranda's mouth there.

"Lash, why don't you free me?"

Because I think I'm going out of my fucking mind, he thought.

"It's so dark in here. I'm so scared."

He hesitated.

"Lash, you are the only one who can save me."

Lizzie stirred.

He shut off the flashlight.

"Lash?" the voice asked, ever so softly.

Lizzie was sleeping on her back, and she tried to roll over, but he wouldn't let her. He pinned her legs down.

"Arrr," Lizzie grunted in her sleep. "Whatchadoin?"

"Kiss me," Miranda said in the darkness.

Lizzie opened her eyes. "Lash? What are you doing down there?"

"Kiss me," said the whisperer.

He moved his mouth close and kissed her. Felt her lips against his. Felt her tongue enter his mouth.

"Oh, Lash," Lizzie groaned. "What are you doing?"

He licked at Miranda's mouth and around it. He licked Lizzie too, her labia, her clitoris. He was sloppy in his hunger.

"Oh my god, Lash," Lizzie groaned. "Don't you ever get enough?"

He licked both women, hungrily, greedily.

"Don't stop, Lash," Lizzie said, in a little cry. "Please don't ever stop."

He took turns licking Lizzie, kissing Miranda.

"Shit!" Lizzie cried out. "Shit!"

She bucked against the bed, like some wild horse.

"Lash," Miranda whispered softly between kisses. "Oh, Lash."

CHAPTER FIFTY-SIX

It was windy on the beach, and Lash covered his face with his arm to keep from getting sand in his eyes. Occasionally, there would be a lull in the wind, and he would put his arm down and look around. There was no one else in sight. He went down to the waterline and sat down, huddled in his coat, looking out at the water. He removed his shoes and socks and he wiggled his toes in the wet sand.

It was so nice to get away for a while.

Back in his apartment, Lizzie was awaiting his return.

Doesn't she work anymore? he wondered. Either she's been saving up all her vacation time or she's quit her job. *Now I'll never get rid of her.*

The last few days were a blur. Of sex. Of drinking. Mostly of sex.

Even here, he thought about Lizzie.

About her body, the sounds she made during sex. Things he hadn't thought about in quite some time. He examined everything about her these days, trying to find clues that could tell him if Miranda's mouth was truly real or if he was losing his mind.

All logic pointed to the fact that he was going mad.

He wondered if Lizzie had acquired some strange powers that would enable her to trap another woman inside her body. Like some kind of sorceress. But that was absurd.

Sand hissed all around him. It was a chilly day. The water roared in front of him. He was close enough that the roar filled his ears, but far enough away that all he felt was a light spray and the tide licking his bare feet.

He was wearing an old cowboy hat that he hadn't worn in

years. He had found it in the closet and had an urge to put it on.

He had to pull it down tight on his head to prevent its blowing away.

The past few days, he had been fucking Lizzie continuously. It was furious, passionate, and sometimes, during these sessions, he felt like a man possessed. It was different than the trances he went into when he rolled for clients, because he was always aware of Lizzie and her body. But these experiences felt similar to his rolling trances, because during both, he had a loss of control.

And that scared him.

What scared him even more was this whole Miranda thing. He had felt the mouth sucking on him, or licking him, inside Lizzie's body. It was happening more often now. It was like he was whipped into a sexual frenzy by it. That was one reason why he made love to Lizzie so often. He wanted so desperately to feel the mouth. To see if it was really there.

If Lizzie could entrap another person inside her body, then why couldn't she control his sexual urges as well?

He was sure that Miranda was real. But then he reminded himself of the crazy hallucination he had seen in the bathroom mirror, and he doubted himself.

One thing was certain. If it was Miranda inside her, he had to do something soon. Before it was too late. Before Lizzie's body assimilated her completely and she ceased to exist.

Did he believe in Miranda's captivity strongly enough to try and free her? Enough to take real action?

All of this was impossible, *wasn't it*?

He had been confused for days. Ever since that night when he had left that man he thought was dead and had wandered the streets for hours, even going to Miranda's old apartment in a daze. It felt as if he would never get his bearings back. It was like he was trapped in some strange, disorienting dream from which he couldn't wake.

And Lizzie seemed to be taking full advantage of the situation, using it to gain some kind of control over him. He didn't tell her to leave anymore. It was futile, and besides, he didn't want her to take Miranda away. But he also felt more passive around Lizzie, more willing to let her have her way. Passive, except for the sex. He seemed to explode with a passion he didn't know he had.

He was a puppet, unable to see the strings that moved him.

And what about Cindy? There were still no messages. He wasn't sure if she was back yet, but he couldn't bring himself to call her. Lizzie had told him that she didn't know about any calls from clients, but he could never be sure if she was telling the truth. He knew she was jealous of his clients, too, as she had been of Miranda.

Maybe he should go over there and try to find Cindy. Talk to her. It might do him some good to talk to someone outside it all. Someone he felt he could trust.

No, he couldn't go to her now. Not like this. *What if he were going insane?*

Lash was so caught up in his thoughts that he hadn't noticed the water. He had walked into it up to his waist, soaking his pants.

He shook himself off as he walked back to the beach.

Then he headed home.

As he walked, he remembered his last client. The man had seemed dead when he left. What had happened to him? It was possible that someone with a weak heart might have a problem with the enhancement thing. The intensity of it all could have put a strain on him. Although nothing negative had ever happened during their previous sessions. Lash had checked the obituaries anyway, convinced he would see the man's face there at some point. His death listed as a heart attack most probably.

Did I kill him? Lash wondered, then tried his best to get his mind off it. There was nothing good that could come of worrying about it. Chances were good the man was alive right now and doing just fine. Lash hadn't called an ambulance that night, but maybe a neighbor had. Or maybe the man had simply come out of it in time.

Lash wandered the streets like a somnambulist, just like he had that night. And somehow, he found himself standing in front of his apartment building.

As he climbed the steps, he realized that it wasn't his place anymore. It was Lizzie's domain now.

He was just a visitor.

CHAPTER FIFTY-SEVEN

Lash woke in the middle of the night. He could hear Miranda's voice calling to him from within Lizzie, begging for him to set her free.

He got up and went to the kitchen, where he got the sharpest knife he could find. He stared down at the knife and ran a finger lightly along the edge, drawing a thin line of blood.

Then he went back into the bedroom and turned on the light on his nightstand. Lizzie was a deep sleeper and didn't notice. He wanted to see what he was doing. Lizzie was asleep, her legs spread apart, invitingly, and, from within, Miranda continued to call out to him.

He put his face close to where Miranda was. "I'm here."

"It won't be much longer until she has devoured me completely," Miranda said. "You must free me."

"I will," he said. "Move back, so I don't hurt you."

There was movement in Lizzie's abdomen, as if a human head were suddenly moving around in there. A head that was only visible, moving beneath her flesh, while she slept.

Lash began cutting. There was so much blood.

Lizzie woke up screaming. He stopped cutting long enough to grab one of the empty wine bottles on the floor beside the bed and smashed it across Lizzie's head. She stopped then. It had only lasted a few seconds, but he was terrified that one of the neighbors might have heard.

Then he heard Miranda's voice again, and that terrified him more.

"Lash, please set me free now. Or else it will be too late. I feel myself dissolving in here. Becoming *part* of her."

In a way, he wished Lizzie could have stayed awake. He

imagined her watching as he cut her open, freeing the prisoner within.

Lash sliced deeply, from her vagina up to her navel. It felt weird cutting into another person. He wondered if this was how surgeons felt the first time they operated.

When the incision had been made, he reached inside, determined to pull Miranda out.

He grasped what he thought was her head and tugged. It came out, and, for an instant, her head became a baby, wriggling in his hands. And then, it was Miranda's head, covered in blood, opening and closing its mouth, making strange, hollow noises as it labored to breathe.

Attached to the head were loose strands of flesh, all that remained of what had been Miranda's body, now bonded to Lizzie's insides, and the head itself had become a new kind of organ.

Whatever Lash held in his hands, it was no longer the woman he loved. It was no longer human at all. Just a strange, disembodied creature, gasping for air like a grotesque fish with a woman's face, saying his name over and over.

The more he stared at it, as it moved in his hands, the more difficult it was to determine whether it had ever really been Miranda at all. Perhaps one of Lizzie's internal organs had somehow mutated itself into a replica of Miranda, to trick him into liberating it from Lizzie's body, so that it could have an independent life of its own.

Lash tried to put it back inside Lizzie, but it was too late. The blood just kept flowing, and both he and Lizzie were covered in it.

The head struggled but could not breathe on its own and was clearly dying. It was choking on the air, its movements growing slower and slower, until it stopped moving altogether.

Lash looked at the head in his hands one last time. It was hairless, deformed. With a repulsive parody of Miranda's features.

Suddenly, he was trembling, and somehow made it down onto the floor in front of the bed.

He began to roll across the carpet, banging into furniture.

And then the trance took him over.

CHAPTER FIFTY-EIGHT

When he woke, still on the floor, he had no idea how long he had been there. Hours, perhaps days. He opened his eyes and stared up at the ceiling, and knew the bed was behind his head. And, on the bed, was Lizzie.

He couldn't be sure if what he remembered really happened, and he was terrified to look.

I have to get out of here, Lash thought.

Slowly, he got up off the floor, and then he turned to face the bed.

It wasn't a dream.

He stared at Lizzie's face. It was contorted in horror or pain. Her eyes were glassy and lifeless.

He stared down at her bloodied abdomen. The things he had pulled out of her no longer looked strange to him. They were simply her organs. Loops of intestines. Her liver. Kidneys.

There was no sign of Miranda's head among the bloodied remains. He must have imagined it all. It must have been a hallucination. A psychotic episode.

But, if that were the case, how could he be sure he was thinking clearly *now*?

The sheets were covered with her blood. He hadn't even tried to clean it all up. Now he realized he should. He had killed her and he had to try to get rid of the evidence.

But he started trembling again and knew that if he stayed in this room, he would go into another trance. He could feel it.

He ran out into the hallway, to the bathroom.

I have to get clean, he thought. *And I have to think of a plan.*

There was blood on him. With all that he had done, it would

have been impossible to avoid some of it getting on him. He turned on the shower.

He could still feel himself trembling as the hot water washed over him, as he scrubbed every inch of himself, but somehow he kept himself from losing consciousness. Maybe he was far enough away from her now to resist falling under the spell.

Lash knew that he had to get out of here.

When his shower was done, Lash quickly got dressed, packed a quick bag, and left the apartment. He had to get as far away as he could. Once outside, he took out his cell phone. He had no idea who he should call, but he needed help.

He had to get rid of the evidence. But he knew that if he went back into that room, he would be helpless to do anything.

He stared at the phone and started scrolling through his address book.

The first person he thought of calling was Joselyn, for some reason. He thought back to that weird session he had done for her. With that strange, hard-faced man. He was almost certain that someone had died that day. That he had contributed to that death, had probably intensified the agony.

But he couldn't be sure.

The nature of the trance he went into meant that he wasn't aware of what really happened, despite his suspicions. Despite what he had overheard afterward.

Part of him said these were shady people who had done terrible things. And if he called them, they might be able to help him dispose of a body, no questions asked.

But another part said, *What if I'm wrong? What if I misinterpreted the events of that day? And, if not, then what makes me think I can trust these people?* And what would they think about him calling them to help him now. Would it tell them he knew what they'd done, that he was a liability after all?

No, Lash thought. *Too many variables there. Too much of a chance it could make things worse. I can't call Joselyn.*

Then he thought of Dasko. The one person he could trust, no matter what. If he called Dasko and asked him to come here and get rid of Lizzie, he knew without a doubt that his old friend would do it, would do whatever it took to help him out.

Lash was tempted to dial Dasko's number, but couldn't. He couldn't involve his friend in this. After the atrocity he had committed, even Dasko couldn't be counted on to keep his secret.

It was then, examining his options, that the phone rang.

He stared at the phone as if it were some alien device he had never used before, then pushed the button to answer the call.

"Lash?" came the voice on the other end. "Lash, is that you?"

"Yes," he said, recognizing Cindy's voice.

CHAPTER FIFTY-NINE

L ash felt a wave of relief wash over him.

"I'm so glad it's you," he said.

"You are?" she asked. "Nice to hear. Sorry to call so early, but I just figured I'd go to voicemail if you didn't pick up."

"I'm here," he said, grateful to hear her voice.

"Lash," she said. "I don't want to complicate things. But I really want to see you."

"I want to see you, too," he said. "Right away. How about I get a cab and come over there right now?"

"So soon?" she asked. "Sure. That would be great. I'll be waiting for you."

He hung up.

Considering he had no other plan, this seemed as good as any. He didn't dare go back into the bedroom, and he didn't know anyone he could call to get rid of the body.

So it made sense to run away.

He called the local cab company and said he would be waiting in front of a nearby convenience store.

He was never going back in that apartment again.

CHAPTER SIXTY

Cindy opened the door and grabbed his arm. "Come on in," she said.

He let her lead him inside.

"Do you want anything to eat?" she asked.

"Sure," he said. "Whatever you've got."

"I was just making breakfast," she said.

He followed her into the kitchen. It was a large room, and in the middle there was a counter with a white marble top. On the stove, he could see she was in the middle of making eggs and bacon. He wondered if she normally did this. It didn't seem like the kind of food she would normally eat. And he thought that she would probably hire people to do the cooking around here. Probably some kind of macro-biotic chef who prepared perfectly healthy meals. Not bacon and eggs. He figured she must be cooking this because she knew he was coming over.

"Would you like coffee?" she asked him, as she finished cooking.

"Sure."

The kitchen opened onto a patio where a table was set for two. He walked out there and sat down at one of the fancy wooden chairs that surrounded the table. It was an unseasonably warm day.

"I had no idea you would be coming so soon," she told him. "Like I said, when I called, I had second thoughts when I heard the phone actually ring. I had no idea what time you woke up, and I didn't want to cause any problems. I almost hung up. If you hadn't answered when you did, I probably would have."

"I was just about to call you," he said. "It was like fate."

"I thought you'd be sleeping."

He thought about Lizzie's mutilated body, and the disfigured head he had found inside her and thought, *How the hell could I sleep?* For a second he saw the patio covered in blood, but it passed, and he was back in reality again.

"I haven't been sleeping much lately."

"That's too bad. I have some sleeping pills if you need them." He could tell she was nervous. Here it was, midmorning, and she was asking if he wanted to get some sleep.

"Not right now," he said. He sat back in the chair and looked at her. She was like a breath of fresh air in his life. "It's so good to see you again."

"I was thinking about you while I was gone," she said. "I was gone longer than I thought I'd be. I kept wanting to call you this past week, but I wasn't sure if I should."

"Of course you should have," Lash said.

"What about your girlfriend," Cindy said. "Miranda?"

"We broke up," Lash said. "It's been a rough time the last few days."

"Remember, the last time we talked, I said there was something I needed to discuss with you?"

"Yeah."

"Can we talk now?" she asked. "I mean, I know you just got here and everything."

"No big deal," he said. "What's the problem?"

"No problem, really," she said. "I just have a confession to make. I've been interested in you for a while now, ever since that first time we met at Antony's place."

She poured him a mug of coffee. He put some sugar and milk in it.

"All that time, I was trying to figure out how to get to know you, but it was complex. First, I was seeing Antony. And then we broke up and weren't talking. I guess, with all that going on, I wasn't ready to pursue someone new, especially if they worked for Antony. I guess, if I wanted to badly enough, I could have found a way to contact you, but there was just so much going on."

"I was attracted to you right away, too," Lash said. "But I didn't know how to pursue it, either. I wasn't sure if you were involved with Antony, and then things got kind of crazy in my own life. I just didn't have a chance to act on it, either. Besides, you and Antony traveled in different worlds than I did, and I had no idea you were even interested."

"Really?" she asked.

She took a long sip through a straw in her glass. She was drinking something that looked exotic. Some kind of daiquiri. It made him want to put some whiskey in his coffee. But he didn't bother to ask.

Their conversation was so mundane. So normal, that it grounded him. Gory images continued to float around in his head, but he was able to keep them at bay.

"Well, anyway, when Antony and I were on speaking terms again, one of the first things I asked him about was you. I wanted to hire you; I figured that would be a good way to meet again. Antony was having his big party around then and told me I should ask you myself."

She handed him a plate with on omelet on it. He ate while she talked.

"That's why I came on to you when you came over here," she said. "I know you probably didn't normally do that kind of thing with your clients. But I wanted to be more than just a client."

"I think you might have achieved that pretty easily," he said. "The last few times we got together were pretty unforgettable."

"But I wasn't sure what my next move should be, when you said you were seeing someone…" Cindy said.

"Like I said, that's all over now."

"I guess what I want to say is I'd really like to have you around as much as possible, and I would love for things to become more serious between us."

"Me, too. We're in agreement about that. So how was your trip, anyway? I think you said that someone had died. I hope it wasn't too painful."

"It was my father," she said. "We were never all that close, I guess. But it did hurt. Luckily, I have a big family and my brothers and sisters were able to make it a lot easier than it would have been. I have a hard time handling stuff like that.

I couldn't wait to get back here. Going home always depresses the hell out of me, and my father's funeral just multiplied that."

"I hope you don't mind me bringing some of my stuff with me," he said, indicating his suitcase on the floor. "I don't want to appear too forward. But I'm having some renovations done to my place, and I can't stay there right now."

"No, not at all," she said. "In fact, I would love for you to stay for a while, if you want to."

"My apartment has too many bad memories," he said. "I needed to have some changes made. But I wasn't sure if you'd want me to stay, and I didn't want to be presumptuous. I guess it was an impulsive thing on my part. I could always get a hotel room or something."

"No," she said. "Please stay here. Have you been lonely at your place now that your girlfriend left you?"

"Yeah," he said, then thought about it. "When Miranda left me, I guess it kind of freaked me out. It was all so sudden. My ex-wife dropped by for a few days, to help me out, I guess, but I've been having a hard time dealing with her. She's been trying to use my breakup to get back into my life, and she's really good at playing mind games. And I guess I was kind of vulnerable. I just had to get away from everything. When you called, I was thinking of leaving, but I didn't know where to go. When I heard your voice, I knew where I wanted to go. I mean, I really wanted to see you again. When I hadn't heard from you in a while, I debated calling you, or coming over here, but I wasn't sure if I should."

"I'm glad everything worked out so well," she said. "It really does feel like fate."

"It was great to hear your voice again. When you called, it kind of put things in perspective again for me."

"I'm glad," Cindy said. "I'm glad I could cheer you up. It sounds like we've both been through some rough times lately. Thanks for being so honest with me."

She seemed genuinely happy.

"What's your ex-wife like?" she asked.

"We stayed kind of friendly after the divorce," he told her. "But I have to admit, she kind of scares me. It's like she's obsessed with me. And I have no idea how to deal with her."

He thought of the last time he had seen Lizzie. Split down the middle with her organs hanging out. And all that blood.

"That's awful," Cindy said. "I have an ex-husband who is kind of like that. I haven't seen him in a long time, but I keep expecting him to pop up one day. He really scares me, too."

"I didn't know that," he said.

"Yeah," Cindy said. "It's not something I publicize. Well, you know, you can stay here as long as you want."

"I have a better idea," Lash said. "You're just getting over a tough time, and I'm eager for a change of scenery. I was thinking, how about if I go to the bank tomorrow and take some money out, and we both take a trip somewhere. Just you and me. We could both use some fun, couldn't we? That is, if you can get away."

"Can I?" Cindy asked. "Of course I can. That sounds wonderful! Just what I need after what's been happening lately."

"Great," Lash said. "I feel the same way. I need to get away for a while, and it will give us a chance to really get to know each other."

She rubbed his leg with hers under the table. Lash finished eating. He finished his coffee.

"Want a refill?"

"Sure. How about putting something extra in it this time?"

She smiled. "Oh shit, I didn't even think to ask if you wanted something a bit stronger."

"Don't worry about it."

Giving his mug back to him, she touched his hand.

"We have so much to do if we're going to go away," she said. "Do you have your passport and everything?"

"Sure," he said. "I'm all set to go. Do you have any suggestions where our destination should be?

"I know this little island," she said. "Almost nobody knows about it. I think you'd really love it."

"Sounds exactly like what the doctor ordered," Lash said, taking a deep drink of what was mostly whiskey. Before she had called, Lash had been on the verge of a panic attack, but suddenly he felt more relaxed than he had in days.

CHAPTER SIXTY-ONE

Cindy was just finishing her packing when the elevator doors opened. Lash was back.

"We'll be using a private jet," Cindy told him. "It belongs to a friend of mine. Everything's all set. We'll be there by tomorrow morning."

"Great," Lash said. "I'm really happy that you want to do this. I can't wait to go to some exotic paradise with you. It sounds like a dream come true."

Thinking of Lizzie alone in his bedroom, he couldn't help thinking of Cindy as his savior.

She laughed and kissed him. It was a long, lingering kiss, and would have led to something else, except they were in a rush and had to keep moving.

"Did everything go well at the bank?"

"Yeah," he said. "Everything went just fine."

He had taken some of his money out of his account, but not enough to close it out, and he had exchanged most of it for the currency of the island they were going to. Of course, there was some cash under the mattress back in his apartment, but as far as he was concerned, that was lost forever.

"Should we call a cab?" he asked.

"No, I've already ordered a limo," she said. "It knows what time to come. Everything's under control."

"You done packing?" he asked.

"Just about. How long do you think you want to stay there, anyway? We can stay as long as you want."

"Can we play it by ear?" he asked. "I really need to get away for a while, but I'm not sure how long."

"Sounds great," she said. "We'll be totally free. No timetables, no responsibilities."

He hadn't packed much in the way of clothes, because most of his clothes had been in the room with Lizzie's body. After he went to the bank, he had done a little shopping and gotten enough clothes and accessories for a few days. Even another suitcase for it all. He had been able to take some cash when he fled the apartment, but the truth was that he was all set. He had money to burn. Once they got to the island, he would get himself a whole new wardrobe. He didn't even need the money he just took out of the bank. The bulk of his assets were in offshore accounts Antony had helped him set up. He had been saving it for years, without knowing what he was saving it for. Well, now he knew.

And the way Cindy lived. The lavish lifestyle. It was all something he could definitely get used to.

"The limousine should be here in half an hour," Cindy said, looking at the wall clock. "You still have time to escape, if you want."

"Escape?" he asked. "I thought that's what *we were* doing. Escaping. I wasn't aware that I had to escape *from* you."

"I was just testing you," she said, and kissed him again.

Despite his happy exterior, Lash was full of anxiety. He felt it was a race against time whether they made it to the airport without incident. He half expected the cops to show up at any moment and take him away. He hoped Cindy wouldn't realize how worried he was, but he found himself biting his lip. He wouldn't feel totally comfortable until they were out of the country.

"This is going to be so much fun," she told him. "Don't be so nervous. We're going to have a great time!"

CHAPTER SIXTY-TWO

"What's wrong, Lash?" Cindy asked.

He was looking out one of the plane's windows and had grown increasingly quiet. "Huh?"

"Something's bothering you," Cindy said. "You were doing a good job hiding it back on the ground. But it's more evident now. Want to talk about it?"

"There's nothing to say."

"I don't believe that."

"I guess it's been a crazy few weeks. I've got a lot on my mind. All the more reason to get away, I guess. I really needed a break from it all."

"I'm flattered you came to me," she said. "I was hoping we were growing closer."

He thought back to the airport. While they were checking their luggage, he had expected security to detain him and police officers to show up at any moment to arrest him, but it hadn't happened. Hopefully, nobody had discovered Lizzie's body yet.

Now, they were flying to some distant island destination he hadn't even heard of before.

Somehow, he had gotten away.

He wondered how long Lizzie could remain in his apartment undetected. There was a good chance she could be there for days, until the smell made discovery inevitable.

He realized he was caught up in his thoughts. It was obvious something was wrong. Cindy was hugging him. "Are you sure you don't want to talk about it?"

After all she had done for him, he felt he had to give her *something*.

"I think I might have killed someone," he said. He was still looking out of the window.

"Really?" Cindy asked him. He could tell she wasn't sure how to react. The decadent rich prided themselves on being hard to shock. But Cindy was different. In order to get her to accept it, he would have to sell her on it.

"He was a client," Lash said, turning to look into Cindy's eyes as she sat beside him. "When I left, I'm not sure if he was breathing anymore."

"Were you sure?" she said. "It can take a lot out of a person."

"I don't know," he said. "I've always been afraid of the possibility of rolling for someone who had a bad heart or something. Maybe this was finally it."

"You can't hold yourself responsible," Cindy said. "You couldn't have known if that was the case."

"I know. And I know that what I do is not an exact science. I can't really control it. *It controls me*, when it happens. There's nothing really I could have done."

"Exactly," Cindy said. "What did you do afterward? Did you call 9-1-1?"

"I was in a kind of fog myself. I remember wandering aimlessly for hours. Or at least it seemed like hours. I haven't been myself lately. It all started that time I found Antony, hanging like that. I fell to the ground and started rolling against my will. Ever since then, I've felt *corrupted* somehow. Like I'm channeling death now, instead of pleasure. That I'm a game of Russian roulette to my clients now. It's the luck of the draw whether I get them off or knock them off."

"All this because of one incident? Because of something that could have had nothing to do with you?"

"I don't know," Lash said. "I haven't been feeling well lately either. It's like there's something foul inside me, gumming up the works."

"Is this why you wanted to run away?"

"Partly," Lash said. "But it's also because my life has been falling apart lately. Too many people leaving me, too many things going sour. I needed to feel like I still existed. That I still mattered. That's why I came to you. I knew you'd find a way to make things good again."

She kissed him. "I'll try, Lash."

"How much longer until we get there?" he asked.

"Another couple of hours," she said. "It's far from civilization. Hardly anyone knows about this place."

"It sounds wonderful."

"My family has had a house on the island since I was a kid. We used to go there during the wintertime when I was growing up. As far as I know, it's been abandoned for the last couple of years. It will be nice to go back there again. I have a lot of good memories of the place."

Lash smiled. It was the first time he had seemed happy since takeoff.

"You want a fresh drink?" she asked him.

"Sure."

It was amazing how spacious the private jet was. How comfortable.

"So what do you want to do for the next couple of hours?" Cindy asked, handing him a new gin on the rocks.

"I don't know," he said. "You got any ideas?"

"You ever join the Mile High Club?" she asked with a sly grin.

"Yeah, years ago."

"You want to rejoin? The dues are even better this time around."

"Sure thing," Lash said. "But no pads. I'm not ready for that yet."

"Okay," Cindy said. "We'll do it like the common people."

They both laughed.

And then they started undressing each other.

CHAPTER SIXTY-THREE

The island was just the way Cindy had described it. From the back deck, he could see the otherworldly turquoise of the ocean. The almost-white sand of the beach. It was like everything in his life had been leading him here.

Or maybe he just felt an incredible rush of relief to be so far away from what he had done to Lizzie. To feel safe again.

The sky was just as brilliant blue. It was midday. He just stood there, staring.

"Pretty breathtaking, huh?" Cindy asked behind him. She was unpacking her things. He had totally forgotten about his own luggage. It could wait.

"This place is beautiful," he told her. "I'm trying to adjust to the reality that we're here. It seems like a dream."

"Doesn't it?" Cindy said. "This place just has that effect on people. I've been here lots of times, and it still has the ability to amaze me. Compared to the city, this is another world."

"Thank you for suggesting we come here," he said. "For *bringing* me here. I can't even begin to describe what I'm feeling right now."

"Well, I'm just glad you're so happy," Cindy said, coming up from behind him, putting her arms around him. "You *are* happy, aren't you?"

"And how!"

"Want to go for a swim?" she asked him.

"Sure," he said, and turned to the bed, where his suitcase was still untouched. "But I better get unpacked first."

"There's no rush," Cindy said. "This is the perfect time to go in the water. It's nice and warm around now."

At her insistence, he had bought a bathing suit when he had

stocked up on clothes before their trip. He dug in his suitcase for it and started to undress.

"You really don't need it," she told him. "There aren't that many people on the island, and the people who are are very casual about these things. People sunbathe on the beach nude all the time."

"You may not have a problem with swimming nude," he told her. "But I'm not as free as you are." He noticed his love handles as he slipped the bathing suit on. His body was changing. He had always been so thin and fit, and now he was filling out.

"I don't see any reason to be so modest," she told him. "You look just fine." She laughed as he looked at himself in the bathroom mirror.

"I could stand to lose a few pounds."

"Couldn't we all," she said, and put her arms around him again.

"You kidding? You look perfect."

Saying that made him think of Miranda, and the extremes she went to keep herself thin. He thought of that night when he had found her bent over the toilet, forcing up her dinner. And how it had aroused him. How strange that had made him feel.

"You know," she told him. "We could stay here forever if you wanted to. My father was a very wealthy man, and I inherited this place when he died. I own a nice chunk of this island. And we have more than enough resources to keep us happy here for a very long time."

He looked at her face in the mirror. "Why are you doing all this? Why me?"

"Because you're the one I want, silly," she told him. "Because I want to share all this with you."

"Now this really seems like a dream," he told her. "I just hope I never wake up from it."

"Come on," she said, walking away. She grabbed his hand and tugged him out of the bathroom, toward the sliding glass doors that looked out onto the ocean. She slid the door open and pulled him out onto the deck again.

"The sand is hot," she told him, as they walked down the stairs to the beach. And it was hot, but after the initial sensation of heat, he really didn't feel it much. He was too busy being aware of *her*.

She was wearing thong bottoms and was topless. The way she looked now, he had never seen her so beautiful before. To be here in this place, with her, was just too much to believe. It would take a while for it to sink in.

They ran across the hot sand to the waiting water. And he had never felt so indestructible and immortal in his whole fucking life.

CHAPTER SIXTY-FOUR

Lash was walking along the waterline, where the sand was coolest. Cindy was back on the beach near her house, sunbathing. After taking a swim, they'd gone back to the house to make love. And now she was sunbathing and he was walking. And thinking.

He couldn't believe his luck. His life was back on track. Lizzie hadn't ruined him after all.

He didn't know how long he had been walking, but, even though Cindy told him that her property line stretched fairly far, he noticed that, as he walked farther along the shoreline, there were other houses. Other people stretched out on their private beaches. He was glad he had thought to put on his bathing suit before heading out for a walk.

He saw a woman stretched out naked on a blanket not far from him and turned to go back the way he had come, when she sat up on her elbows. She was wearing sunglasses and a large, floppy hat. He forced himself not to stare.

"Lash!"

He stopped in his tracks. How could he have stumbled upon someone else he knew out here, so far from civilization?

She got up and ran toward him. "Lash, is that you?"

He still didn't respond. As she approached, he realized who it was. *Joselyn.*

"Yeah, it's me."

"I was sure it had to be a mistake," she said. "What are you doing out here?"

"I came with a friend," he told her. "I needed a vacation."

"You couldn't ask for a nicer place to get away to," Joselyn said. "But I didn't think anyone else knew about this place. A friend of mine owns the house and told me to come out here for a while. I have to admit, if I knew it was this beautiful, I would have taken him up on his offer a long time ago."

He couldn't help wondering if she had come here because he was here. It made no sense, and he knew he was being paranoid. But he had a tendency to think that way.

"Yeah, it's a great place."

"You have to come in for a minute," she told him. "I'll make you a drink."

"I can't really stay. Someone's expecting me. I was walking much longer than I should have been."

"You can stay for one drink, can't you?"

He looked her over. She was just as pretty as he remembered. If he didn't have Cindy waiting for him, he would be very tempted by her, despite the strange session he had had over her place a month before. When he was sure someone had been murdered in her apartment. Part of him wanted to get as far away from her as possible. But another part was thirsty and wanted that drink.

"Sure," he said. "One drink couldn't hurt."

He followed her back to the house she was staying in. She didn't make any move to put on any clothes, but she also did not seem to be trying to seduce him. It was like she wasn't even aware of her nakedness. He couldn't help feeling a bit aroused, and it embarrassed him.

"I was wondering if I'd ever see you again," she said, making his drink. "You didn't return my phone calls. Is gin on the rocks okay?"

"It's just fine," he said, taking the drink from her. "Sorry about the phone calls. I'd been going through some rough times, and kind of lost track of things for a time."

"Nothing too rough I hope."

"Rough enough. But it's all over now. I've got a fresh start."

"You wouldn't be interested in rolling for me again, would you?"

It was kind of unexpected the way she just jumped into it so quickly. They had barely gotten inside.

"I don't know," he said. "I'm kind of retired from that."

"Please," she said. "I'll pay you well. Just one more time, for old time's sake?"

He thought of Cindy, begging him to put on the pads and roll with her. Would it ever be safe to do it again for her? Or would he always be afraid that if he did, he would hurt her somehow. *Channel some death her way.* She had seemed understanding enough, but he wanted so badly to make her feel ecstasy again.

And here was Joselyn, out of the blue, offering him a chance to test his ability out again, and see if it was safe.

There was a chance he could hurt *her*, too. But it didn't seem as important.

"For old time's sake, huh?"

"Please?" Joselyn said. "Won't you at least consider it?"

"Yeah, sure. I'll think about it."

"We're having some people here tomorrow night. If you decide you want to do it, just come back here then, around ten. Do you have a number I can reach you at?"

"I don't know it," he said. "And I don't have my cell phone. If I decide to do it, I'll just show up."

He drank from his glass. She moved closer.

"Please decide to come," she said. "I'll make you very happy you did."

"I'm considering it."

"So who are you staying with? Is it someone I know?"

"I don't think so," he said. There was no reason to tell her about Cindy. Not now. Sure, they knew each other, but Lash felt protective of Cindy. He didn't want to involve her in this. Just in case his suspicions about Joselyn were real.

"You're so secretive," Joselyn said with a laugh. She ran her fingers through his hair playfully. He resisted the urge to stop her. "This is the first time I've ever been here. Isn't it an amazing place?"

"Sure is," Lash said.

"Joselyn?" a man's voice called from another room. Probably her friend who owned his place. The voice sounded familiar.

"Harry," Joselyn said. "I want you to meet a friend of mine. His name is Lash. Imagine meeting someone I know all the way out here."

"That *is* pretty amazing," the man said, coming into view. He was big and burly and maybe in his late forties or early fifties. That seemed to be Joselyn's type, if he remembered correctly.

Lash didn't recognize the man's face, but he recognized the voice. It was his old client, Corporate Man. The one who always wore a mask. He had never seen the man's face before, but he would never forget that distinctive voice. That made Lash think of the girl he had been with last time, the one he had nicknamed Peroxide Girl.

The same girl who he was sure had died in Joselyn's apartment.

He saw recognition in the man's face too, but he still pretended to be a stranger.

"I'm Harry Ramsom," he said, thrusting forth one of his big hands. "Nice to meet you."

Lash took the hand and shook it, not missing a beat.

"I was trying to talk him into coming to our party tomorrow night," Joselyn said.

"That's a great idea," Harry said. "Can you make it, Lash?"

"I'm going to try."

"We'd love to have you," Harry said.

"He has some really interesting talents that I'll tell you about later," Joselyn said. And Lash wondered about their upcoming conversation, after he had left, where Harry would no doubt tell her that he was already aware of Lash's *talents*.

"Well, thanks for the drink," Lash said. "But I've really got to be going."

"Don't forget about tomorrow night," Joselyn said, taking the glass from him. "We'd really love to have you."

"Sure," Lash said. "Nice seeing you again, Joselyn. Nice meeting you, Harry."

"Same here, Lash."

Joselyn walked him to the porch. Before he went back onto the beach, she said to him, "Remember what I said. I'll be *very* generous."

CHAPTER SIXTY-FIVE

"Where did you go?" Cindy asked when he got back to where she had been sunbathing. "I was worried you'd disappeared."

"I just went down the shoreline a bit. It's a longer walk than I thought."

"I fell asleep," she told him. "And I got burned."

"Not too badly, I hope," he said, kneeling down beside her.

"I hope not, too," she said, gathering her stuff together. "Let's go inside."

"Yeah," he said. "I'm starting to get hungry."

He carried her blanket and they walked up the beach to the deck behind her house. He looked back. The stretch of beach was completely devoid of other people. It was like they were the only two people in the world.

But not really. He thought back to Joselyn. And Harry Ramsom. Lash had finally seen the face behind Corporate Man's mask.

He resisted the urge to tell Cindy about seeing Joselyn, especially if he was seriously considering going back there the next night.

"Do you ever think about Antony?" she asked him, as she looked through the refrigerator. Somehow, it was full of food, even though they'd just gotten there.

"Where did all the food come from?"

"I have someone look in on the place when I can't be here," she told him. "Kind of a caretaker, but he doesn't stay here. And he takes care of a lot of places on the island. I let him know beforehand when we were coming, and he made sure the place was well stocked."

"Pretty convenient," he said.

"So, answer my question."

"Yeah, I think about him sometimes," Lash said. "I was the one who found him like that."

"I know. It must have been quite a shock."

"It was."

"Did you ever talk to him about things?"

"What kind of things?"

"I don't know. Anything that strikes you as interesting."

"We had some small talk," Lash said. "Never anything too deep. He was a nice guy, though, and one of my oldest clients. I really liked the guy."

"Did he seem especially moody to you?"

"Sometimes. He was kind of quiet sometimes."

"But you're still surprised at what he did?"

"Yeah," Lash said. "He never seemed the type to kill himself. Not really."

"I miss him, too," Cindy said. "But I have to admit, even I never felt like I really knew him. He wasn't the type of person to really talk about his inner thoughts. He kept that kind of stuff private. I wish he hadn't felt the need to hold back so much."

"Some people are just like that," Lash said.

"We have just about everything in here. I was going to hire a chef for our stay, but I wanted us to be completely alone. What are you in the mood to eat?"

"Surprise me," Lash said, and walked out of the kitchen. He wandered down the hall to the bedroom and turned on the television. Some of the shows were in a language he didn't understand. He stretched out on the bed, resting on his stomach, and watched.

After a while, Cindy came in.

"So here's where you went," she said. "You just disappeared on me."

"I'm sorry," he said.

But she could tell his mind was somewhere else. The way he acted, it reminded her a lot of Antony.

CHAPTER SIXTY-SIX

The next day, Lash made sure to stay on Cindy's part of the beach. He made sure not to wander off too far when he went walking.

When he returned to the house, Cindy was still stretched out on the bed.

"Are you okay?"

"I got a sunburn yesterday," she told him. "I thought I'd stay inside today. Want to keep me company?"

"Okay."

"Why don't you make us some drinks."

While he was making them both strawberry daiquiris, he looked at the clock. It was a little after one in the afternoon. He had a lot of time yet to decide whether he really wanted to go to Joselyn's house later that night. He had been debating it since he had seen her. On the one hand, he really didn't want to do it. But he wanted so badly to see what would happen if he rolled again. For some reason, he was really nervous about doing it again.

He brought the drinks into the bedroom. Cindy took her glass.

"I thought you were making these when I heard the blender going," she said. "You know how much I love them."

"Yeah," he said. "I thought it might be nice on a hot afternoon."

"Are you getting bored yet?" she asked him.

"No."

"You can be honest with me."

"I'm here with you," he said. "I don't want to be anywhere else."

"But you were never much of a sun person; you told me that once."

"It's okay. Everything's so beautiful here."

"But any kind of beauty gets boring over time," she said. "Nothing keeps its appeal forever."

"We only just got here," he said. "The appeal hasn't even come close to wearing off."

"I just know you can be restless," Cindy said. "Maybe we should take a trip to the mainland soon, do some shopping. Look around. There isn't much to do on the island if you don't love swimming or sunbathing."

"I'm fine," he told her, drinking his drink. "Please, don't worry about me. I'm happy here. Really, I am."

"Want to make love?" she asked him.

"I thought you had a sunburn."

"I do," she said. "But I'm getting restless too."

"Okay," he said, and finished the rest of his drink.

"I never knew anyone who drank like you do," she told him.

"As long as there's liquor around, and you, I'll be just fine," he said.

CHAPTER SIXTY-SEVEN

"So you actually made it," Joselyn said. "I didn't think you were coming. It's almost midnight."

"I know," Lash said. "I didn't think I'd be able to make it, either."

She looked over his shoulder down at the beach. "So you came by yourself?"

"Yeah."

"That's too bad. I wish you'd brought Cindy along with you."

The look on his face must have betrayed his surprise, because she smiled then. "You didn't tell her about my party, did you?"

"She wasn't feeling very well tonight," Lash said. He instantly regretted deciding to come here.

"Don't worry, I didn't say anything to her. In fact, she doesn't even know I'm here. And we can keep it that way if you want. Me and Cindy go way back, but we were never really what you'd call friends."

"Then, how did you know?" he said it despite himself.

"Oh, I'm really good at detective work," Joselyn said, and laughed. He wasn't sure how to take the laughter. "But don't look so worried, I won't say a word. And I'm actually honored you decided to show up for our little shindig after all. Heaven knows it could use a good shot in the arm."

Harry Ramsom saw him talking to Joselyn and squeezed his way through the crowd.

"Boy, am I glad to see you," he said. "I knew you wouldn't let us down."

"That's funny," Lash said. "I didn't know if I was coming until the last minute."

"Would you like something to drink?"

"Sure."

Harry squeezed back through the crowd to the bar. Lash looked around the room but didn't see any faces he recognized. Most of the people were in bathing suits, and many of the women were topless at this point. There seemed to be little clutches of people here and there, who were fucking or on their way there. Some people watched them, but most were caught up in their own conversations.

"The party didn't quite catch fire like I thought it would," Joselyn said to him. She was wearing skimpy, beige bikini bottoms and some elaborately heeled fetish shoes, and nothing else. He wondered why she bothered to wear what little she did. This was clearly meant to turn into an orgy at some point.

He was surprised when Joselyn even came to open the door. He figured everyone would be occupied by this time.

"I told everyone you were coming," Joselyn explained, "and I gave them a hint of what they were in for. That's why things aren't totally crazy here yet. You don't know anyone else here. Hell, I don't even know most of them. A lot of them are Harry's friends and arrived specially for this party. But they sure are in for a surprise, huh?"

"Yeah," Lash said.

Harry came back with a glass of gin on the rocks. Everyone seemed to know about his gin preference. It made him want to ask for something else. He was becoming too predictable.

"Thanks," he said and took the glass from Harry. "How soon do you want to begin?"

"As soon as you're ready," Harry said. "Everyone's been looking forward to this."

"I'm so glad you didn't stand us up," Joselyn said. "I really had faith in you."

He downed half of the drink and handed the glass back to Harry. "I'm ready. Where are we going to do this, in this room?"

"It's the biggest room in the house," Harry said. "And some people have already started without us."

Joselyn laughed at that.

"Okay, I'm going to need some space. Can you clear a section of the floor for me? And you can tell everyone to get started."

"Sure thing," Harry said.

After he had gone back into the crowd to get things ready, Joselyn handed Lash an envelope. "I know from experience I may not be in the best of shape after this. So I better pay you now. Remember I said I'd make it worth your while? I'm giving you double your normal rate. Don't spend it all in one place." She winked at him.

"Thanks," Lash said, taking the money and putting it in his pocket.

"Attention everyone," Harry bellowed, and the voices that buzzed throughout the room stopped. "Our guest of honor has arrived, and we'd like to get things started. We need to clear some floor space for him."

Lash felt like a performer, and in a way he was. But he did not address his audience. As they cleared out an area for him, he started getting undressed, feeling dozens of sets of eyes on him, keeping his back to them. He hated being the center of attention and liked the fact that once he got started, everyone would be too preoccupied to even be aware of him.

Once he removed his clothes, he got down on the floor. By this time, he could hear everyone else removing what little clothes they had left and getting settled on the lush carpeting as well. Their initial curiosity phase was over and now they were getting ready for what they'd been promised. He knew that many of them had no idea what lay ahead. Not really.

Lash began to roll. It was something he didn't even have to think about at this point. He just let his body go and closed his eyes. Images flashed through his mind, and he had no control over them. Antony hanging from his ceiling. Lizzie covered in her own blood. Cindy in the throes of orgasm. Good and bad images collided and raced through his mind like a current that pushed him forward. He tried to blank his mind, to no avail. The images were just too vivid. This wasn't the way it usually went.

Slowly, the trance took charge and the images faded in intensity, then disappeared completely.

He could hear the sounds of people crying out behind

him, locked in the sensations he was generating. He was like a gigantic sexual battery, charging everyone in the room. The sounds were good, and then the trance took over, and he lost even the ability to hear them anymore.

When he drifted back into consciousness, something felt different. Awareness happened slowly, and each person in the room was a faint ray of light, on the verge of going out, and, in the middle of the room, was a radiance stronger than all the rest. Immediately, he knew what it was. There was a pregnant woman among the revelers, and he could sense the child stirring within her. And, in some strange way, he felt that it was aware of him in turn.

The unborn child's light intensified, growing so bright that his hand instinctively rose to cover his eyes, even though they were still closed, and then the light extinguished, taking all the other lights away with it, sending him back into his trance, back into darkness, as his body thrashed about on the carpet.

When Lash gained consciousness again, he felt himself rolling back and forth, felt the carpet rubbing against his body and face. He was moving so furiously that he was getting carpet burns. Normally, he was very aware of the kind of surface he was rolling on, but this time he had just wanted to get it over with and hadn't bothered seeing how comfortable it would be.

He stopped moving. The room was full of the smells of sex, and something else he could not readily identify. And there was an overwhelming silence.

Lash sat up and turned his upper body to look.

The room was full of bodies. It was a gigantic jigsaw puzzle of human shapes, interlocking and covering the length of the carpet. This was nothing new. When he woke up, he usually found his clients in an exhausted state, unmoving.

But there was blood this time. Lots of it. And some of the faces he saw had a real look of horror on them.

I was right, he thought. *I'm channeling death now. All that death filled me to the brim and it's coming out of me now.*

The room didn't look like the aftermath of an enthusiastic orgy. It looked instead like the inside of a death camp. It was obvious that most of the people had died in agony. Whether or not it had started out as pleasure, at some point, it all turned to pain and ugliness.

It was then that he remembered the vision he had had, of the pregnant woman in the middle of the room and her fetus. He did not know its significance, and he was not about to go searching for the woman's body in the sea of limbs and torsos. Besides, he knew it was too late to save her.

"Fuck," Lash said, finding his clothes and hurriedly putting them on again. He felt the envelope Joselyn had given him, folded and bulging in the seam of his pants pocket. When he was dressed, he made his way for the door.

He passed Joselyn. She was stretched out on the carpet, unmoving. She had a weird expression etched into her face. Somewhere between ecstasy and a scream.

Harry was close by, his limbs locked around another woman. Both of them were contorted into impossible shapes that must have broken bones. Several of the faces he passed were smeared with blood, as if they'd just thrown up their insides.

Lash ran out onto the back deck, and the roar of the ocean outside made him stop for a moment. It was like the scene inside the house had been some kind of cruel nightmare, and the night air brought him back to reality.

He turned to look back into the room he had just left, and nothing had changed. It wasn't a dream at all.

Lash ran down the steps of the deck, to the sand of the beach, and then he just kept running, until he couldn't run anymore.

CHAPTER SIXTY-EIGHT

"Where have you been?" Cindy asked when he got back. The sun was starting to rise on a new day.

"I couldn't sleep," he said. "I went out for a run."

"I woke up in the middle of the night," she said, "and you weren't here. You weren't anywhere in the house. Did you go running all night long?"

"I had a lot on my mind," Lash said. "I needed some time to myself. Time to think. I certainly didn't mean to scare you. I didn't think you'd even notice."

"Well, I *did* notice," she told him. "And I *was* scared."

He put his arms around her, "Well, don't be. Everything's just fine. Are you feeling better? I know you weren't feeling too good last night."

"You don't like it here, do you?"

"I know I've been kind of restless, but I've never been one for the beach, is all. I don't like to swim and there's only so much walking I can do."

"We do other things," she said.

"I know," he said. "It's just all so new to me."

"Maybe we should go somewhere else."

"I don't know," he said hesitantly, and that room came back to him, a vivid image of mass death. And a child like a sun that burned itself out.

"So you *don't* like it here!"

"I need a shower something fierce," he told her.

"Lash, I wish you'd talk to me. I wish you'd be honest with me."

"I am being honest," he told her. "I honestly need a shower."

He left the room. Cindy could hear the shower running. She

wanted so badly to get him to open up to her, but he only gave her glimpses of the real him. Never enough to really hold on to. Never enough clues to really figure him out.

It was then that the doorbell rang.

Cindy went and closed the door to the bathroom. They'd gotten so comfortable here that they never shut doors anymore. And then she went and answered the front door. It was a police officer. He said he was with the island police. She hadn't even realized the island was big enough to warrant its own police force.

"Excuse me, ma'am," the man said. He was dressed in a shiny blue uniform and was clearly uncomfortable in the heat. "Could I have a word with you?"

"Of course."

"Did you happen to know the people who live in the next house."

"We've only been here a short time," she told him. "I didn't even know we had neighbors. I mean, I know there are other people on the island, but we've been keeping to ourselves."

"I know the houses are pretty far apart," he said. "So you don't know the gentleman who had the next house over. A Mr. Ramsom? Harry Ramsom. He was an American, too."

"No, the name isn't familiar. Why? Is there a problem?"

"I just came from his house," the officer said. "It's quite horrible. It looks like they were having a party. But everyone is dead."

"Oh my God."

"It's quite a horrific sight," the man said. "I've never before seen anything like that. Normally it's pretty quiet on the island."

"I know. That's why we came here."

"So you're not here by yourself, ma'am?"

"No," Cindy said, realizing too late that maybe she should have kept Lash out of it. "I'm here with my fiancé."

"Is he available? I'd like to speak with him, too, if I could."

"He's in the shower. But I can tell you we haven't left this house in days, except to use the beach out back. Neither one of us ever met the neighbors. We only just got here."

"So he wouldn't have known them either."

"No."

"They're examining the bodies now. There's suspicion that drugs may have been involved. I'm only asking around as a formality. Just to see if anyone knows anything. I know this is a small island, but we do have crime here, believe it or not. Drugs, mostly. Nothing that normally involves violence, you know, but wherever there are rich people who want a good time, dealers are going to find customers. But there are some new synthetic drugs going around. We think this was one of them with some nasty side effects. Just between us, it looked like a pretty wild party over there. Things obviously got out of hand."

"Well, my fiancé and I are new here," Cindy said. "We don't know anybody else."

"That's fine," the officer said. "I am sorry to bother you. As I said, this was just a formality. I know the houses are so far apart, it can seem like they're worlds away. I have been asking everyone on this side of the island if they'd heard anything. Seen anything. I was hoping someone might have a clue as to what happened to those poor people."

"It does sound horrible," Cindy said.

"I'd never seen anything like that before," the man said, clearly still shaken. "It throws a real scare into you, seeing so many dead people in the same place."

The man ran a hand through his hair. He was perspiring profusely, and Cindy felt a few drops of sweat spray onto her as well.

"I am sorry to bother you," the man said. "I am glad you and your fiancé are unharmed. This is an awful way to welcome you to the island. I've seen enough tragedy to last me the rest of my life."

"Sorry I couldn't be of any help," Cindy said, and watched as the man walked down the stairs of the deck and back to his car. It was an old police car, probably inherited from mainland division that had upgraded.

The man climbed into his car and drove away.

"What was that about?" Lash asked.

"A police officer," Cindy said. "The people in the next house over were found dead this morning. A whole bunch of people, from the sound of it."

"Any idea what caused it?"

"He said something about a bad batch of drugs. It sounds pretty scary to me." She stared into his eyes. "Lash, where were you last night?"

"Cindy, I told you…"

"Lash, please. I told the man you were with me the whole night. That we knew nothing about it. But if you do know anything, I want you to tell me. I don't want any more secrets between us. Not now."

"Okay," he said. "I was there."

"Tell me what happened."

CHAPTER SIXTY-NINE

"Remember I told you that something weird happened before we left the States? That I thought someone might have died because of my rolling?"

"You said that you weren't sure about that," Cindy said. "But that the man could have had a weak heart and didn't know it."

"That's possible," Lash said. "But the truth is, things have been getting weird for me ever since I found Antony, when he hung himself."

"What do you mean?"

"When I found him, I rolled around on the ground uncontrollably. It was beyond my control, and I couldn't stop it until it stopped itself. I have never felt so helpless before. Like some kind of puppet. The way it felt, it was like I was channeling death."

"You said that before," she said. "But it doesn't make any sense."

"Well, there was another time, when some clients of mine did something horrible to a girl they'd hired to join them."

"Oh, Lash!"

"I can't be sure. I was in a trance. I don't remember anything. But afterward, when I woke up, everything was so strange. And there were traces of blood."

"Did you call the police?"

"How could I?" he said. "I had no evidence anything bad had really happened. And I had no idea how to explain what I was doing there, even if I did know for sure."

"But what about the blood?"

"That could have been anything. It didn't necessarily mean someone had died."

"So what happened then?"

"After that, my rolling has been unpredictable. Sometimes, everything goes fine, but other times, like that man who I think died, I have no idea. I don't know what I'm doing anymore when I go into those trances. What the end result will be."

"Were you rolling last night?" Cindy asked. "At that house? Where all those people died."

"I had to be sure that everything was okay again," Lash said. "I wanted so badly to do it for you. Like that time when we used the padding. I wanted things to be the way they used to be. I've been feeling so weird lately. But I didn't dare test it out on you. There had to be another way."

"How did you even meet the people over there, and how did you tell them what you could do?"

"They already knew."

"What do you mean?"

"I was walking along the beach, I guess I've been kind of restless, and I stumbled across our neighbors. It's a pretty long stretch between your property and theirs. The houses on this island are very far apart."

"I know. That's why this place is so exclusive. Total privacy. And everyone around here has enough money to keep it that way."

"Well, I came across the people over there. And I knew the woman. It was Joselyn."

"*Antony's* Joselyn?"

"Yep."

"Imagine that. What are the chances we'd come across people we knew way out here? Why didn't you tell me you'd bumped into Joselyn?"

"Because I didn't trust her. I even suspected that she had followed us here."

"Followed us? What are you talking about?"

"I'm probably wrong. It was probably a total coincidence. But it just kind of unnerved me. You see, I was at Joselyn's that time, when I was sure that girl had been harmed."

"Joselyn? I know she's into some kinky stuff, but is she really capable of hurting someone?"

"I think so. I really do. Or at the least, she allowed someone to be harmed. She arranged for it to happen."

"But you're not sure."

"I told you what kind of effect that night had on me, on my rolling. It felt a lot like the time I'd found Antony. It was too similar to just ignore."

"So you really think Joselyn helped murder someone."

"I think it's a very real possibility," Lash said. "Which is why I didn't tell you she was on the island, and why I didn't say anything to her about you being here."

"So why did you go over there last night?"

"I told you. I had to find out if the bad shit I'd channeled was still in my system. I wanted to see if things were back to normal again. I was sure that, given enough time, I'd be just fine again. But I didn't want to risk anything with you. So when I saw Joselyn, she asked me to come back the next night, for their party. She was staying with another client of mine, some guy named Harry Ramsom."

"The police officer mentioned him. The name sounds vaguely familiar, but I don't think I've met him before."

"He used to wear a mask during our sessions for some weird reason. He didn't want me to know who he really was. But I couldn't miss that voice anywhere, or his build. He's a big bear of a guy."

"Was he at Joselyn's house that time the girl was killed, too?"

"No. It wasn't him. But the girl, I'd seen her before. At one of my sessions with Harry."

"That *is* weird," Cindy said.

"There were definite links," Lash said. "And it was clear to me Harry was aware I'd figured out who he was, but he didn't seem all that upset that I'd finally met him without his mask. In fact, he seemed pretty cool with it."

"So they asked you to go back, for their party?"

"Well, they both know what I can do. I think they assumed I wanted the money. And I told you I needed someone to test my theory on. That I was okay again. And you weren't feeling well last night, anyway."

"And you slipped over there when you thought I was sleeping."

"Sorry about that. I really didn't expect any of this to happen. And I didn't want to involve you. Although I assumed Joselyn would show up over here at some point, if the rolling went well. She was always trying to see me as much as possible after Antony died."

"So what happened over there?"

"I rolled, and things got really weird again. And when I woke up," Lash stopped for a moment. "It was pretty bad."

"That policeman was obviously freaked out by what he saw."

"I don't blame him."

"So you think you're still *channeling death*, as you call it?"

"I was last night, that's for certain. But I have no clue if it will happen again, or if I got it out of my system."

"So you can't roll for me anymore?"

"Not if I don't want something awful to happen to you."

"Well, I don't know if that police officer will be coming back," Cindy said. "He seemed pretty convinced that we had nothing to do with it. But you can never be sure. He might come back to talk to you. I kind of let the cat out of the bag that I wasn't here alone."

"I just wish it hadn't happened," Lash said. "I wish everything had gone normally. I really thought it would by now."

"So we just have to be like normal people, that's all. No enhanced extras," she said. "It's not the end of the world."

"It is for Joselyn and the rest," Lash said. "You sure you're not freaked out by all this?"

"Of course I'm freaked out," Cindy said. "But we'll have to deal with it. At least now I know what this is all about. You have to be straight with me, Lash. At all times."

"If I'd told you about Joselyn, would you have let me go over there last night?"

"I doubt it. I think there's a good argument that you shouldn't have gone."

"Yeah," Lash said. "But I was going to do it anyway."

"Should we be thinking about leaving the island?"

"Maybe," Lash said. "It could look suspicious if we just up and go. Then again, it could just be that we're scared and we don't want the same thing to happen to us."

"That's true," Cindy said. "It could look either way."

"I need a drink," Lash said.

"It's not even noon yet," Cindy said. "Maybe you should cut down on that stuff."

"Fuck that," Lash said, going to the bar and filling his glass with whiskey. "After what I saw last night, I need a drink something fierce."

"Well, let's go get something to eat. We haven't been to town yet. There's a small shopping area in the center of the island. Might as well go exploring for once, especially if you're getting restless."

"Okay," he said, between gulps of his drink. "I'll tell you, I won't be able to get that scene out of my head for the rest of my life. And the worst part of it is, I caused it, whether I meant to or not. I killed those people.

"And there's something else. One of the women there, at the party, was pregnant. I just know it. I saw a vision of her fetus, when I tried to come out of my trance the first time. It scared the hell out of me. And I feel horrible about it. I never would have gone over there if I'd known."

"What do you mean, a vision?"

"I can't explain it well," he said. "It was a powerful image. And it had a very strong effect on me. But I'm not sure what it means."

CHAPTER SEVENTY

A warm breeze wafted in through the open bedroom window. Lash woke and looked over at Cindy. She was sleeping beside him. Her arms hung over her side of the bed. They were both naked. It was hot, and they didn't need sheets.

He thought about the day they'd just spent together. He was suddenly familiar with the feeling of being in love again. He had thought he would be too jaded to ever experience that again, to really feel it. But it turned out that such things weren't beyond his grasp after all. They'd gone to town, shopping and getting a bite to eat. Simple things, actually. But there was something about the two of them, holding hands like kids wherever they went, sneaking kisses when the other one wasn't looking, that made him feel downright giddy. Lash didn't remember feeling like this in a very long time.

He could see the moon from where he lay. It was three-quarters full and very white. It filled the room with an otherworldly glow.

He moved slowly, carefully, as not to wake Cindy. He rearranged the pillow behind him, so that he could sit back and watch the moon better. He wanted to take it in. And take *her* in. His eyes kept shifting from the moon to her asleep. He felt strangely good.

He thought about his life. About how things had changed since he and Cindy had come to this place.

He had used her as a way out, that day at the airport. But she had been so game to go along with it. She wanted to take off and start over again as much as he did.

Now that they had time to really get to know each other, Lash found that he and Cindy actually had several things in common. Things he would have never guessed at.

She had been divorced, too. Her ex-husband had been rich, but abusive. He had been almost as obsessive as Lizzie. But Cindy had had the money to move around. To escape.

She told him, when they first got to this island paradise, that she had been living in the city too long and was getting too set in her ways. She was getting anxious that her ex-husband might come back into her life sometime soon. That he might invade her peace. So she had had her reasons for leaving the country, too.

She had dreaded telling him. Because she thought it was a heavy burden to lay on someone she had been seeing for so short a time. But the events of the last two days had shown he had heavy burdens of his own. And that didn't even include Lizzie, who never left his thoughts. Who haunted him always. He told Cindy some things about Lizzie, about her obsessiveness, and the way she had tried to keep him in her life. But he didn't tell Cindy everything. Like how she died. There were some things he had to keep to himself.

She told him that, in his arms, she had felt safe, really safe, for the first time in years. And, tonight, she fell asleep in his arms.

During their day trip, she had confessed that she had fallen in love with him a while ago. That first time they'd made love, she was already head over heels.

It was funny. *Head over heels.* No one had ever said that to him before.

It was a calm love. A peaceful love. Not like Lizzie's obsessive hunger, her psychotic needs. Not like Miranda's cautious love, always maintaining a distance, always keeping secrets and hiding unspoken fears.

No, Cindy was different. She was relaxed with him. She confided in him.

But it wasn't all peaceful. Their passion was a storm between the calms.

He had told her about Miranda. How she had simply disappeared from his life one day without explanation. How he had missed her a lot more than he thought he would. And how, even now, her leaving baffled him. She had just moved into his place, and they were just on the verge of something meaningful, when she changed her mind and went away.

He tried to explain to her what it felt when he went into his rolling trances. But it was hard to put into words.

She told him that, with the death of her father, she was the beneficiary to an immense inheritance. She could buy this whole island if she wanted. And if things got uncomfortable here, they could go anywhere else in the world they wanted to go.

He wouldn't have to roll on the floor for anyone ever again if he didn't want to.

They'd already started talking about where they could go, just for a change of scenery, until things on the island got quiet again. Tomorrow, they planned to take the short flight to the mainland. There was a casino there, which sounded like fun.

As he sat there, resting against a big, fluffy pillow, watching the moon hang before him, he thought of Miranda. He never did find out where she ended up. It was like she had disappeared off the face of the earth. It didn't matter now, but he was curious. He couldn't imagine anything Lizzie might have said that could have set her off enough to leave so abruptly and completely. They had been happy together, if just for a short time, and then she had seemed so angry at the end. Anger that didn't make sense to him.

He thought of Lizzie. The way she kept turning up at his apartment when he least expected it. And how she died. And the more he thought about it, the more he was convinced it hadn't happened at all. That it had been some kind of bizarre hallucination. It seemed so real, and her mutilated corpse haunted his dreams, *but it couldn't be real*. He kept telling himself that whenever he worried that her body would be found.

And then he would remember what it felt to hold a knife in his hands and cut through human flesh. It had seemed real enough.

Real or not, the images of her death never left him.

And he thought of that beach house full of dead bodies that he had caused with his rolling. Blood everywhere. Hands twisted into claws. Faces that were grotesque masks of pain.

Somehow, they did not seem to be under suspicion. The policeman had not returned. He hoped they would be content with their theory of tainted drugs. Cindy was already making plans for them to leave the island in another day or two.

He thought about his old life and realized he had no desire to go back.

He had everything he wanted here, with Cindy. He had to block out the images, the ghosts that haunted him.

Lash looked over at her, and it made him smile. The way she slept. She looked truly angelic. He had heard people described that way before, but it never fit anyone like it fit Cindy, at that moment.

Then he thought of her face caught up in sexual passion.

She was definitely no angel.

And he was glad of it.

Despite the horrors he had recently witnessed, he felt strangely contented. Here, with the woman he loved. He tried to block out everything else that had ever happened and focus exclusively on her. She was what was keeping him alive right now.

He moved to get out of bed, and she reached out for him, pulled him close, and before he even realized it, they were making love.

CHAPTER SEVENTY-ONE

The casino turned out to be a lot more exciting than he had expected. They had spent most of the time at the roulette table and were ahead in the game. A large crowd had gathered around the table.

"I'm really glad we decided to come to the mainland," Cindy told him. "Are you having a good time?"

"Sure," he told her. "This was a great idea. I might go play some poker later."

"Do whatever you want," she said. "Enjoy yourself."

It was then that Lash noticed that one of the women in the crowd was waving to him. He didn't recognize her at first, but then it slowly dawned on him. It was the college girl he and Dasko had double-teamed back home. He was slightly embarrassed by the memory and hesitated before he waved back at her.

What's she doing in a place like this? he wondered. *Halfway around the world.*

"I'm so glad you remembered me," the girl said, approaching them. She was wearing a long, beautiful white dress and her hair was styled up on her head. She looked completely different now. She looked like some kind of movie star.

Lash found it difficult to believe this was the same girl he had had sex with during that drunken binge. But it was definitely her. He realized he didn't even know her name.

"I would like to introduce you to my friend, Mr. Marx."

There was a tall man beside her. Lash could not be sure of the man's age, but he had long, white hair in a ponytail behind his head, and was dressed impeccably in an Italian suit.

"Harry Marx," the man said, shaking his hand. He had a

very firm grip. "You and your wife here just won me a lot of money at the table. I wanted to thank you. When Katrina told me she knew you, I begged her to introduce me."

"Very nice to meet you," Lash said. "And this isn't my wife, but she is my fiancée. Cindy, this is Mr. Marx and Katrina."

"An old friend," Katrina said with a giggle.

"I was just telling Lash here that your lucky streak was beneficial to me as well," Marx said. "And I wanted to thank you both."

"No need to thank us," Cindy said.

"Not at all. I would love for you both to come up to my room for a drink. I have a wonderful view of the ocean."

"Why not just go to the bar?" Lash said. "It's just over there."

"Because I would like to talk to you both. Katrina has told me so much about you. And it's very difficult to talk down here."

What could Katrina have told him? Lash wondered. *I barely even know her.*

"I think it would be nice," Cindy said. "We need a break from gambling, anyway."

"Okay," Lash said. "Lead the way."

Katrina giggled again and took Marx's arm as they walked toward the elevators. Cindy and Lash were also dressed to the nines and everything seemed so elegant here. Lash felt a little out of his element, and he still found it hard to trust anyone, but this was Cindy's world. He decided to follow her lead on these things.

But it still baffled him what a girl like Katrina would be doing here. He wondered if maybe she was a high-priced escort.

If so, the kid's doing pretty good for herself, Lash thought as they got into the elevator.

Marx pressed the button for the top floor and the elevator rose silently but quickly.

"Are you both staying here as well?" Marx asked.

"We were thinking about it," Cindy said. "We actually hadn't planned that far in advance. We're staying on one of the nearby islands and just flew over here for the day."

"I have a big suite," Marx said. "The entire penthouse. There's plenty of room. You two could be my guests."

"We certainly wouldn't want to impose on you," Lash said.

"Not at all," Marx said. "I would actually welcome the chance to thank you for your good luck. It would be my pleasure to have you as my guests."

Lash felt a little weird about this. He wasn't used to making friends with people so quickly, and it was all going a little fast for his taste, but Cindy seemed calm enough.

The elevator doors opened and they walked down a short hallway to a door painted gold. Marx swiped his card to open it and led them inside.

When he turned on the lights, someone grabbed Cindy and pulled her away, covering her mouth. Someone else injected Lash with something that immediately put him to sleep.

CHAPTER SEVENTY-TWO

When Lash finally woke up, he found himself naked and lying on his back, inside of a weird metal cage. Someone was shaking the cage violently.

Lash sat up and looked around. A big, mean-looking guy in a suit had been doing the shaking. He stopped once Lash moved around. But they were not alone. There were about ten people in the room, in various stages of undress. Marx was stretched out on a bed, behind the cage, and Katrina was at his side.

"You're finally awake," Marx said. "Now we can have some fun."

"Do what you did before," Katrina shouted.

I don't remember rolling when we were with the girl, Lash thought. But then again there were several gaps in his memory when it came to the drunken weekend at Dasko's. There was no reason why he *wouldn't* have done it. And Katrina clearly wouldn't have forgotten something so earthshaking.

"What am I doing in a cage?" Lash asked.

"I collect unusual pets, Mr. Lash," Marx said. "And you're the latest addition to my menagerie. I suggest you cooperate if you want to see your fiancée again."

Something in the way Marx said it made Lash wonder if he would ever see Cindy again. For all he knew, she might be already dead. He didn't see her anywhere in the room.

"Roll around on the floor for us!" Katrina shouted.

"I suggest you do what lovely Katrina requests," Marx said. "My guests are growing impatient and I have promised them a special treat tonight. I certainly hope Katrina wasn't wrong about your skills."

"No," Katrina said. "He can do it. You'll see."

The big guy in the suit approached the cage again. "You heard Mr. Marx. Start doing your thing."

The man stuck something in between the bars and Lash received a violent shock. It was a cattle prod of some kind.

"Do it!"

Lash got down on his back again. The cage gave him just enough room to roll around in, but he was sure he'd bang into the bars while in his trance. But he didn't see that he had any options. He closed his eyes and began to roll back and forth.

He hoped that Marx and his guests would suffer the same fate as Joselyn's island party, but even as he hovered on the verge of his trance, Lash could feel that there was no more death inside him. He had channeled it all out of his system on the island.

The trance, as it enveloped him, filled him with a sense of bliss as he lost consciousness.

A bliss he had never felt before.

ABOUT THE AUTHOR

L. L. Soares is the Bram Stoker Award-winning author of the novel *Life Rage*, published in 2012. His other books include the shared short story collection *In Sickness* (with Laura Cooney), and the novels *Hard* (also published by Crossroad Press), *Buried in Blue Clay*, and the one you're reading now.

His fiction has appeared in such magazines as *Cemetery Dance, Horror Garage, Shroud,* and *Gothic.net,* and in numerous anthologies including *The Best of Horrorfind 2, Wicked Weird and Zippered Flesh: Tales of Body Enhancements Gone Bad!* Volumes 1-3. For more than a decade, he co-wrote the movie review column Cinema Knife Fight, which was a finalist for the Bram Stoker Award in 2009.

To keep abreast of his most recent endeavors, check out his website at www.llsoares.com. He lives in the Boston area with his wife, and an iguana named Osiris.

Curious about other Crossroad Press books?
Stop by our site:
http://store.crossroadpress.com
We offer quality writing
in digital, audio, and print formats.